The

Elk Killings

Rick Mansfield

The Elk Killings

This book is fiction, as are all the characters; and except for the elk mutilation, any resemblance to real events or real people is purely coincidental.   Information about CWD is, however, based on knowledge at the time of printing.

Dedication

This book is dedicated to my dear friends **Bill and Sue Terry** of Jadwin, MO; as well as to all who have by direction and example passed to the next generation the principles of fair chase and sportsmanship that He would have us to exercise in our dominion over His creation.

I owe much to their friendship and support and am eternally grateful. Thanks!

Acknowledgements

As always, I am grateful to my wife and helpmate Judy for being the light and warmth of my life. She continues to be the earthly rock that gives me strength.

I wish to thank my neighbor and good friend, Mrs. Verna Moss. Her editing and encouragement make my writing possible, the final product better.

I thank Minit Print of Poplar Bluff for their cover design, as well as Debbie Dakin of The Licking News for an important proof fix.

I also wish to recognize those that try to provide for and protect our wild game. These include farmers as well as law enforcement agents, true hunters as well as honest outdoorsmen. When Man was given dominion over these animals, it came as well with responsibilities.

"There can be no greater issue than that of conservation in this country."

Theodore Roosevelt

"I seek the solace of the woods as often as I can; for the sinful nature that pervades the world of man makes me weary. The serenity of Nature restores me."

C.W. Nichols, 1900's River guide

Chapter One

It was very much like the morning before; and for that matter, the one before that. Winter had only recently completed her job of baring the trees of all their foliage; the last of the withered messengers having traveled from limb to forest floor. A sky devoid of all but the smallest clouds allowed the sun to go about unheeded in its task of warming the south-facing Ozark hill. Cedars with brown trunks were interspersed among the decades old stand of lighter and larger white oak. Two, nearly a hundred yards apart, had served for rubs as the bulls strengthened both necks and antlers in preparation for the rut which had ended scarce weeks ago. These stood out, as now exposed inner bark shone in the rays of the sun, making them appear as matching gateposts to an entry to an almost magical place.

Almost magical as it was the frequent haunt of a small herd of elk that took refuge amid these side hollows when not grazing in the bottom fields adjacent to the river. A herd only recently repatriated into an area from where they'd been extinct for more than a century and a half. It was here that I came as chance would allow. It was here that I shed the minutia that took far too much of my days and helped me to reconnect with the strength that was the outdoors; that again steeled me for the seemingly endless reviews of contracts and legal descriptions that I dealt with daily. It was mornings such as this that I treasured.

But not this morning; for it was not like the mornings before; nor would this place ever be the same again. Not for me. The magic was gone. The scene before me was an emotional punch in the gut. I had hoped to catch a glimpse of the elk, maybe even one of the magnificent bulls that had made the aforementioned rubs. I had never considered the horror I now saw. There before me was one of the mature bulls; quiet in death. A quiet that belayed the act that had taken place; for not only was the animal dead but its marvelous antlers removed along with a significant portion of its skull. Brown leaves were covered with the gory aftermath of the heinous act. No, this morning was different; as were my feelings toward this once serene piece of forest. My name is Rachel Hunt. I felt now somehow forever changed.

Chapter Two

A calm had finally settled over me; more a sense of deadness than peace. Years of chronicling the flora and fauna of the outdoors in which I'd grown guided me as I took both pictures and notes documenting the crime I had just uncovered. As much as I dreaded the embarrassment this was sure to bring to what many of the urban parts of the state considered ignorant "hillbillies;" nevertheless, I knew this had to be reported. It was to the local conservation office I now was headed.

I had followed closely the now five-year-old project that had introduced this largest member of the deer family back to a region it had roamed for a millennium. In my part-time role as outdoor writer, I had done numerous articles documenting its progress; had taken hundreds of photographs. Had watched as the herd had grown to more than one hundred animals, a full dozen of which were mature bulls. Six of which were "royals"-- males with antlers of six points on each side. One was considered an "imperial" with the ends of each antler forming a "Y" with a resulting 7 x 7 rack. It was this animal I feared dead, as the remaining carcass would easily weigh in excess of eight hundred and fifty pounds. Maybe nearer a thousand.

Even before exiting the vehicle, I had glimpsed the tawny hide from the road. Taking the route I normally took when hiking through these particular woods, I had gone nearer the animal. Had felt a physical repulsion when first viewing the carnage. Had walked part of the trail that in mornings past had taken me alongside the two rubs. Took note of the presence of acorns beneath the mature oaks; well aware that these animals preferred the grasses and legumes in the nearby fields, quite unlike their smaller white-tailed cousins.

I knew there had already been a few casualties. Some calves eaten by the mountain lion population the Conservation Corps still insisted was only a few transitory males migrating through the area on the rarest of occasion. One large bull that died of disease. The original releases had been on Conservation property where access was more easily controlled. To cultivate public support for a project that had passed expenditures of more than a million dollars, viewing opportunities were increased commensurate with the growing of the herd. It was then the rumors began.

The first was that government workers had butchered one of the young males for the meat. This came from a scene found by some hikers where obviously a large animal had been skidded across the forest floor. There was not much blood, but a couple of squirrel hunters had later said the skid path was far larger than for any white-tail they had ever seen harvested in these parts. The next came from some canoeists. They told the vendor that later picked them up they had seen what they believed to be a slaughter site near one of the shoals they had floated past on their weekend adventure. There had been others, none of which could be traced back to original sources. Rumors based on rumors mingled with supposition and speculation. More than once, I had tried unsuccessfully to track them down. The Corps always refuted any such stories; insisting there had been no poaching to date.

Like most of the people from the small rural community in which we lived, I applauded much of the efforts and successes of the Conservation Corps; while at the same time questioning some of their practices and attitudes. A long-standing joke about the state bureaucracy was that if there were five employees present there were probably six vehicles. Still, aside from a few farmers and hunters; the vast majority agreed to the repatriation of the majestic animals. Increased tourism in the falls was already being linked to ever increasing sightings of the growing herd. I could not help but wonder what this poaching incident would mean. Such were my thoughts as I pulled into the parking lot of the Corps' district office.

Chapter Three

"I'm not real comfortable with the press wanting to accompany us to the site." This from James Middleton, the Corps' resident "elk expert." And after I had provided them with exact GPS coordinates as to the location of the elk, and after having shown them I had already taken pictures. I was not sure how much of his attitude was directed towards me and how much was grandstanding for his fellow employees and the young intern forever at his side. Molly Roberts was in her senior year of high school, and after a summer of wearing the T-shirt of a Corps volunteer, was now part of an internship for advanced placement students dual enrolled in our local college satellite. Classes were taught at the local high school in the evenings and generally by the same staff teaching the secondary courses throughout the days.

I was also unsure of what I found more offensive; the affront to the rights of the press or the characterization of me as merely "the press" when I spent much of my time and even financial resources preserving the area's environment. I viewed myself first and foremost as a conservationist and resented the lack of recognition of such status.

"Well, since I am a member of the press and the animal is on public property, I will be driving back out there." As I had intended, my statement left little room for negotiation. I left them with the directions; arrived onsite first. Other than the typical borderline dysfunction of most government employees, the process went as I had anticipated. The animal was skidded down to the road and then loaded into a pickup truck for transportation to their state offices for a necropsy. As of now, the only known crime was the unauthorized removal of the antlers from the deceased elk. Removal, officers surmised, done by a chainsaw.

I photographed the process, which not surprisingly, took far longer than expected. The morning turned to late afternoon. I had an energy bar in my coat pocket, a canteen of fresh water in my truck. My Golden Lab back at home, however, would be expecting supper in just another hour. I made my questions brief. They made their responses briefer.

"Is this the first case of poaching, if in fact this elk was killed and did not die of natural causes?"

"This is an active investigation and the Corps does not comment on such." Middleton was at his obtuse prime. And again, I could not help but wonder if this was meant as much to impress young Ms. Roberts, who had remained a constant at his side, as it was typical bureaucratic obfuscation.

"Will there be additional resources other than the regular county agents assigned to the case?"

"This is an active investigation and the Corps does not comment on such."

"Will there be a press release when the necropsy is completed?"

"This is an active investigation and the Corps does not comment on such." Again.

I persisted with questions directed at the agents themselves, but Middleton injected himself into each attempt with the same rehearsed reply. Once, one of the four agents began to respond, but was quickly cutoff by Middleton. I thanked them for their time and headed back to my small townhouse on the edge of town. I had a canine companion needing to be walked and fed. I looked forward to his company, as well as some possibly more stimulating conversation. Rex was a talker!

Some Alpo and Hamburger Helper later, not entirely sure which of the two had been more thoroughly enjoyed; I uploaded my photos to my computer. I had some good shots, albeit the gruesomeness of the subject. My favorite was one of somber reflection on the part of three of the employees as the carcass was first drug to the road. The most graphic actually showed the ravaged skull.

I filed first with the editor to whom I had already tested the waters for interest; the non-profit newspaper that actually credentialed me as a full-fledged member of the Missouri Press. I then posted several photos and a few notes to my website that generally gathered a few hits of interest each evening; strongly believing that the sooner the public was made aware, the sooner someone might recall particular traffic in the area or some other tidbit that would lead to a successful prosecution. With the public on notice, perhaps someone would remember who had a chainsaw in their vehicle, though with winter hunting camps this would not be that uncommon. In the next few days, my words and pictures spread across a state mostly outraged by the crime.

And a crime it was. The necropsy had revealed the animal had in fact been shot. Numerous organizations were pledging reward money to help bring the perpetrator to justice. My spare time was being consumed with phone calls requesting interviews, my sense of indignation playing better than the oft rehearsed, "This is an active investigation and the Corps does not comment on such." Besides, I also had pictures.

The majority of my days were being spent utilizing the dual degrees I had earned years ago while still trying to figure out what I wanted to be when I grew up. Turns out a glorified accountant. Both lawyer and CPA, I was fast becoming the "go to gal" for all things financial and contractual, especially when dealing with ore and timber rights. It would be the coming weekend before I could go once more to the river and the surrounding hills. Not sure of where I would in fact go, or for what I would be looking; the woods became much more crowded long before I had a chance to decide.

Chapter Four

The call came from a gigger. Taking advantage of a series of cold nights partially clearing the stream colored from recent flooding, they went out in search of one last mess of yellow suckers to fry. Traveling downstream before dusk, planning on gigging back up after dark; they saw it. Or them, for it was a gathering of buzzards and crows that first attracted the men's attention.

Initially they believed they had found another elk, for the recent poaching event was foremost on most everyone's mind. What they found was far worse. For though the illegal taking of game was an abomination to all sportsmen; the taking of human life was much worse. And that is what they found displayed on the gravel bar as the winter sun was setting behind the ridge to the west. Murder.

Leaving one of their group behind to guard what was once a living being; the other two hurried back upstream to get cell service. It was then the owner of the boat made the 911 call. It would be almost an hour before law enforcement arrived, transported by that same boat that had originally made the discovery. A very long hour for the man that had remained behind. A man that had seen far more than he had wished; the image of the eyeless skull and the pale body bloated from death one he would wish to erase many, many times in the coming years.

Most small-town papers are printed but weekly; the appetite for news much more avarice. Internet postings on Facebook, tweets and emails complemented the website coverage of the nearby urban papers. Rampant speculation filled the gaps left devoid of facts.

There had been but one reporter on the scene, a retired serviceman that wrote for one of the local papers. Free-lanced for some others. Catching the call on the radio he kept tuned to local law enforcement, and having his own Blazer river boat; he arrived shortly after the law. As the gigger ferried first county deputies and then a Conservation Corps warden down the river, the Corps' own boat sitting back at the office on a trailer with two flat tires, the reporter just stood back and watched. Took no pictures, asked no questions. This was far from his first crime scene. This time, no one said a word about the presence of the press.

Within less than a day the story was out there. The victim identified was none other than the Conservation Corp's own James Middleton. Misinformation was assuredly fueled by the now absence of the agency's local de facto spokesperson. His role with the department and the fact that his eyes had been removed gave birth to the belief that he had intentionally been blinded for what he had seen; what he knew. This complementing the belief already held by some that somehow certain members of the Corp were profiting personally from the restoration project. The constant secrecy and benign press releases only added to such assumptions.

With the twenty-four-hour news cycle constantly needing to be fed, eventually the pictures of the decapitated elk resurfaced. Initially shoved to a back burner by the murder of a state employee; it had remained alive in part because of the vicinity of the crimes as well as the ever-increasing reward offers raised by various conservation and environmental groups. The more calloused of the local communities noted there was more monetary reward to be had by identifying the killer of the elk than that of the elk expert.

There were some facts out there. The body of the elk as well as that of the state biologist had been found less than a mile apart. The antlers and skull cap had been removed from the elk; the eyes from the man. The first most probably done by chainsaw. Contrary to the ready assumptions of the general public; the second actually by crows, the soft tissue of the eyes a favorite of carrion feeders. Both post-mortem.

There were a lot of unsubstantiated stories as well. The removal of the eyes by the murderer. The cadre of state employees personally profiting from the project; the state itself conducting experiments in secrecy. The stories of earlier cases of poaching in the area. Even the "games."

The majority of the community were at least vaguely aware several local teenagers had conducted competitions earlier in the fall. Spotlighted whitetail and only took the horns. Later contests had them only cutting off tails to verify their kills, targets now including does as well as bucks. Winter's cold had slowed the practice if town gossip could be believed at least in part. That was where the mystery stood less than a week from the original crime.

Chapter Five

Mark Williams had been with the National Park Service for more than thirty years; his retirement available whenever he chose. Today he was wishing he had already turned in his badge and gun; was in another state fishing. Mark knew about the young men from surrounding communities that had been killing and leaving deer to rot, all for the sake of numbers. He had even spoken to one father when talk had reached him about a particular evening.

"Know all about it," was the father's response. "But my kid was too drunk to shoot that evening. Nearly passed out while driving home!" The fact that his son was driving a motor vehicle under the influence had not seemed to bother the man; nor had the boy's participation in trespass and poaching. Since the incident was outside Mark's jurisdiction, he pursued it no further. In fact, the majority of the carcasses found in recent winters were outside the national park in which he did have authority--to an extent.

The rules of co-operation with the state dictated that Park Rangers could write citations under state law, but the illegal killing of game was still considered a misdemeanor even when taken under spotlight and thus carried little penalty even when enforced. Local prosecutors and judges were elected, and the prevailing winds unfortunately blew against enforcement.

Mark realized there had always been an almost innate disrespect for authority in this area and for the men and institutions that were charged with the protection of game. It was just that the more recent trend was not only a continued disrespect for those whose job it was to protect the game, but an almost total lack of respect for the game itself. Animals were left to rot; sometimes without even the back straps or hams removed. Wounded animals were no longer tracked, but left to agonize and die on their own.

He had often wondered that if the culture of the Native Americans still remained and hunters believed each animal had its own spirit, would such practices have ever been begun? There was a time, not that long before these magnificent animals ceased to roam this river valley in the midst of the 19th century, when prayers of thanks were offered each and every time such an animal was harvested. The Spirit gods were thanked for the food, shelter and clothing the animal's sacrifice would provide.

As a Christian outdoorsman himself, he did not understand it. He had been taught that man's dominion of the birds of the air, fish of the sea and over "every living thing that moved on the earth" came with great responsibility. Game was to be taken "in fair chase" and within the regulations established by the state. "Render unto Caesar what is Caesar's" meant adherence to man's law as long as it was not in conflict with that of God's.

Mark had not been contacted by the state authorities; the National Park not called. Not by the Corps. He first saw the pictures on the internet. Was appalled by the atrocity. Days later he was shocked by the murder of a man in uniform. Had to believe the two were somehow connected. He was interviewed almost in passing as he filled his pickup at a local station.

"Know anything I should know?" Sheriff Barnes had inquired. Ranger Williams had to suppress a smile, thinking to himself that information would fill a wagon; perhaps a wagon train.

"No, Joe" he responded respectful of the position. "Not on this" he could not help but edit. Joe nodded; either approval or dismissal—it was hard to tell with the sheriff, who left, cup of coffee in hand.

Over the years, Mark had developed a small group of confidants; people with whom he could speak in confidentiality. Though holding no jurisdiction over the spotlighting on private properties, he would very much like to solve the elk atrocity and, as a law enforcement officer, certainly wished to assist in the takedown of the person responsible for killing a government employee. It was for these reasons Mark began to decide which paths to pursue. It was his belief in the two crimes' connections that steered him to his next call.

Chapter Six

"He really came to see your father," Ronnie asked his high school friend. The two had been anxious to speak to each other since the mutilated elk carcass had been found, but Scott's afterschool job with his uncle had made their getting together difficult. The recent visitor had made them all the more nervous.

"Yes!" the young man responded almost frantically. "Back before deer season and then again after church last Sunday. Went out to the barn and stayed out there for more than an hour. When I came out they pretended to be talking about cattle." Scott was all but rambling; his speech hurried and face blushed.

"Ranger Williams has cattle, same breed as your dad. Maybe that's all there was to it." Ronnie reasoned.

"Sure..... and maybe they were considering going together on a new hay conditioner, or splitting the cost of a better seed bull for the coming spring." Scott's voice began to climb as he continued. "Or, maybe they were discussing the possibility of us cutting the antlers off of an elk. Maybe the good ranger doesn't believe what our dads told the warden a few weeks ago. Just maybe the law figures us to be involved in a lot more than collecting a few 'tails' and such. Maybe......"

Ronnie cut his friend off mid-sentence. "Maybe we should just calm down. You got rid of the 'stuff' you had, haven't you? You said you had."

"And I did. Speaking of getting rid of things, how did you explain to your father a saw coming up missing? You got rid of it, right? You said you did." Scott had meant for his inquisition to be a blend of sarcasm and condemnation; it came out more like petulance and whining.

Ronnie took a deep breath, using the gesture to calm himself and focus his thoughts; much as when facing a three and two count with bases loaded. Captain of the baseball team for the past two years, he was somewhat used to taking charge in close situations. And with the death of the conservation guy, things were getting close.

"Look," Ronnie mildly decreed, "just keep your mouth shut. Don't say anything to anybody. Not the law; not even your father."

"Don't worry about my dad," Scott began to become defensive. "If I've heard him say it once, I've heard it a thousand times. 'Blood is thicker than water.' He's got my back. Whether a few beers in my truck or caught breaking curfew during season, he'll say whatever it takes to keep me out of trouble. We're cool!"

"Cool or not, don't tell him anything. Look....we need to get to class. We have a lot more we have to talk about. Meet me at the bridge tomorrow night. Sometime late. I'll get there when I can." Ronnie was walking away as he spoke the last few words.

Scott took off the other direction, fully aware of their need to talk and disturbed by all that was going on in his life. He was sure his father had his back; it wasn't his father he was afraid of.

Chapter Seven

Scott ended up not making it to class. His conversation with his fellow classmate had done more to unnerve than calm him; in particular the questions about his father's recent conversations. He knew his father would protect him, always had. From school authorities, from the law. Even his mother, who in the last few years had become increasingly obsessed with her son's behavior. All that "you'll be judged by the company you keep" nonsense. What of the company he kept?

There was Ronnie, captain and best pitcher of the baseball team and one of the more popular kids in school. Always taking life as it came, there were times his aloofness was more irritating than encouraging. Still, he was solid. Unflappable. Ronnie always came through in a crunch. Scott still remembered well the beaning of a kid from a nearby town that had made the mistake of hitting on one of Ronnie's friend's girl. Sent him to the hospital with a fractured jaw. Yeah, Ronnie could be counted on to do what was necessary.

There was his girlfriend Molly. A cheerleader and honors student. He supposed they were still going steady, though this recent evening college class and all the extra hours that went with it were turning out to be much worse than her volunteering last summer. He had planned a whole schedule of fun and she ended up spending all her weekdays running around in khaki shorts he believed "too short" and that silly blue volunteer "T" he knew was too tight.

With his working weekends in the summer for his uncle, they never seemed to have much time together. And when together, she was never romantically inclined. "Dr. Middleton this" and "Dr. Middleton that." Molly insisted all the volunteering and now the class and internship would look great on college applications. Scott guessed all relationships had their problems. Molly was one of the prettiest girls in school and she was his.

Then, of course, there was Buddy of "Buddy's Bait & Tackle" down on the lake. He hung around there when not at work or at school. Helped Buddy with some of his "off the books work." There was always a ready market for fish and game mounts; Scott helped with the illegal fish traps in the lake and the spotlighting of trophy animals in the park.

Scott believed Buddy to be a modern-day rebel. He knew the man did not report much of his legal income from boat rentals and repairs, fishing tackle and live bait. Many of these were cash transactions and never made it to the recorded receipts. But it was his night activities and the games he had instituted that were of greatest interest to the high schooler. Games learned of by "word of mouth" by an entrusted few.

There was the tail game. Buddy gave free beer to whoever brought in the most deer tails in a week. Played the game for three months each fall. It was toward the end of the first year that Scott finally realized Buddy had a market for deer hair. Fly tiers up north; some company in Michigan. From success here, he got involved in the sneaking into the park at night and harvesting trophy deer.

Buddy had a Colt Accurized AR-15 with a sound suppressor and ATN Night Vision scope they had used on their first adventure together. Took a seven-year-old twelve point buck that would score an easy 175 Boone & Crockett when dry. Scott did not get to shoot that first night, but this year had already used the newer Les Baer .223 with a FLIR System thermal vision scope. Scott was impressed with the audacity Buddy showed to sneak onto both private land and into public parks. They had killed deer within feet of people's back yards; had taken one large buck right in a city park.

Scott still played the tail game with Ronnie and several others; killing mostly does just to quickly get their numbers up. Had even invited Molly along a time or two when Ronnie or someone else did the shooting. The "trophy hunts" were with only Buddy. Buddy even slipped him an occasional "C note" for these evenings, especially when they used Scott's truck. Money he used to buy Molly jewelry and things; presents he certainly could not afford on what his uncle paid him at the canoe livery. Money that went well with the funds from their other "off the records" enterprises. Yes, Scott realized that though this was more than likely the "company" his mother was talking about, Buddy had changed his life.

Chapter Eight

I got out of bed before daylight, donned some sweats and wrapping a scarf over my mouth, headed out for a couple of miles. The town was to my left; I turned right. Needed to clear my head. I had been up late trying to figure out where to look for clues with thoughts of board feet per acre constantly injecting themselves into my deliberations; deadlines for some timber bid contracts distracting me. Rex preferred the South Road as it was called.

The town route was usually plenty quiet at this hour; only a few businesses open this early. Generally met shop keepers opening up and fellow joggers and walkers sharing the quiet streets. I enjoyed the comradery of the small town and select group that watched it awake. Sharing a good morning with people I had known most of my life.

But today I wished for solitude, and knew there would be none later at the office. We had a murderer among us; as well as a game thief. Possibly one and the same person, or persons. I even thought as a lawyer while running. The Corps wasn't saying anything; and as my almost daily trips to the courthouse revealed, neither was the sheriff's office nor prosecuting attorney. If there were any good leads, they were not being leaked to the public.

I wanted to help. Not for the glory of "making a bust," but in part to get the bitter taste out of my mouth that was in every swallow. A physical reaction to guilt, perhaps, for even though I worked hard as a volunteer conservationist, in my own way; I had not always reported game violations when I heard about them. I often used the excuse "nothing would be done," which was sadly often the case in that most poaching was at best a misdemeanor and sentences were imposed by judges that had to run for reelection. Sadder still; I heard of these infractions from many of my neighbors who were too often willing participants.

I kept trying to believe that this was different; the level of disdain for wildlife of a greater depth and that public outrage would finally be voiced by all. Or at least most. And then there was the murder. A human life taken no doubt in some way connected to the first crime; misdemeanor or not. I felt that the latter was an inevitable escalation when any society chooses to live, even in part, outside the law.

I had always been a fixer, perhaps because of my status as a middle child; maybe because I grew up a female in a man's world. I had to fix this. I had to do more than take pictures and write pretty articles. But where to start. Maybe it was time to reach out for help; but to whom. These were my thoughts as I stepped into a shower and sensed stumpage figures and production costs reinvade my consciousness.

Chapter Nine

Mark had left the informal meeting quite befuddled. He had known the gentleman with whom he had just spent the past hour for several years; believing they shared much more than simply the same church home. He had believed their mutual acceptance of Christ as Savior had given them a comparable set of values; similar levels of respect for the bounty of Nature present on the very lands they farmed. Bounty entrusted to us as His stewards.

"Coyote bait!" That had been the man's reply. "Should have left it to them and the buzzards" he'd continued. He didn't want to hear about the majesty of the mature bull or the wonder of having elk back in the county after more than a century and a half absence. He railed against his tax dollar "supporting such foolishness" and griped of the threat such a herd was to his farm. Mark felt an almost visceral hatred of the animal on the man's part.

The fellow farmer and church-goer certainly did not wish to discuss the activities of his own child or any of the child's friends. As to a few deer left to rot, "boys will be boys" was the response. Mark could hardly believe this was coming from a Christian father.

He changed topics after only a few minutes, sensing discussion of the murder would be received as further allegations against the man's son. They talked farming; how such a wet spring and summer had so quickly become a dry fall. Speculated about snowfall for the winter that had just begun.

"A man's dead" he'd remarked as he finally turned to leave. "That won't go away. I'd appreciate a call if you hear anything." They shook hands and parted. The farmer remained in his barn as Mark walked back to his truck. Somehow he sensed that their next meeting at church would be a little less cordial; that their friendship would be strained until this entire affair was behind them. Wondered if such a thing was really ever possible; if the taking of a life ever left any community the same.

Mark Williams was a deliberate man. That is why three days later he was reliving that conversation in his head. He had helped to catch poachers before, through patience and persistence. Believed now much more to be at stake. Knew from experience that almost any predator once having tasted human flesh had to be put down; for it was too prone to repeat the experience. Wondered if the same was true of man. Was this simply a case of escalation? First deer, then elk; and with the threat of exposure— man? What had James Middleton known that cost him his life? Who had he suspected? Who had he scared? Such were his thoughts as his radio came to life.

Chapter Ten

Buddy Stevens was a reprobate. He knew it; his parents had known it. Neighbors attending their funeral believed the little good that could be said about the house fire that took both their lives was that not only was smoke inhalation a fairly painless death; they had not had to live to see the shame brought upon their family name by their only child. In his thirties at the time of their death, Buddy had inherited a promising boat business, some cabins and the bait and tackle shop. The shop barely a mile from the lake was all that was left; the rest borrowed against and lost in the first two decades following the tragedy. There was the store itself and one storage shed out behind that.

He had briefly worked for the county, hired by the man preceding the current office holder in the sheriff's department. Had actually even worn a deputy's badge for over a year. Hung around weathering numerous complaints long enough to file for disability based on a wrenched back, supposedly from wrestling a suspect one evening.

It was hard to tell if Buddy really knew what most of the community thought of him; for people purchasing his legitimate offerings were generally only there on weekends and knew him as a somewhat affable, if prone to constant bragging, outdoorsmen.

Most honest adults that lived there full time had little interaction. They bought their supplies online and caught their own bait. Knew of far better marine mechanics not that far from town.

Buddy's friends consisted mostly of adolescent males, many still in high school. Acquaintances he had made from young men hanging around during those frequent after-hours times when he broke open a case of beer and worried not a bit about the age of the young people imbibing. Comrades he introduced to his nefarious endeavors at a multitude of different levels; all somehow contributing to Buddy's bank accounts.

There was the tail game he had started to access an abundant supply of deer hair for both legitimate and illegal buyers. The frozen gamefish he provided for out of towners seeking a "wall fish" of which they could display in their urban offices and homes, constantly detailing their personal prowess in the creature's capture. These often caught in illegal traps and nets.

There were the trophy mounts for the same type of individual. Men with money passing themselves off as sportsmen when they did no more than purchase an animal they could then have stuffed. Buddy preferred the "client" to transport the kill to the taxidermists themselves; he trying to remain somewhat under the radar as to the actual number of mounts he was selling. When necessary, he would do so but for an additional fee. Here was where he had found big money, and here was a trade few knew about; at least locally. Anything that would score 160 points on the Boone & Crockett scale was bringing him five thousand dollars a head. A really great whitetail rack in the 175 plus range often fetched twice that amount.

At present, only the one teenager knew of this particular sideline. Had actually assisted in the harvesting, if taking the game illegally at night and then cutting off its head and cape could be called a "harvest." Buddy had even let the kid fire the shot one night, though usually it was the boy's job to cut off the head with horns after Buddy had sufficiently caped back the hide past the shoulders.

People in the big city knew. Just as for centuries soldiers learned of foreign brothels and thieves knew where to sell their illicit goods, word had spread among those interested where a trophy could be had; sufficient with backstory so that heads could be displayed and tales told with little fear of truth entering the picture. This past fall alone, he had sold seven such prizes.

And there remained, of course, his oldest source of illicit income. Drugs. The same kids that enjoyed an illegal beer were easily enticed into trying something "with more of a hit." And then the chosen of these became conduits into many of the local communities. At present, he had no less than five such souls working for him. Popular kids that believed Buddy was their benefactor, while in reality there was not a soul in his life he did not consider expendable.

Divorce had taken a wife and two children, the result of one of his few attempts at some level of normalcy. The new vehicles and ready spending money had not been enough for her to continue to look the other way. Not when she could see in her children the very same disrespect for anything of intrinsic value she had finally come to see in her betrothed.

What few times investigations had begun a path the least bit near to him, Buddy had found a way to sever the lead. Once an anonymous tip had even netted him a couple of hundred from the states Operation Game Thief. He spent all of it buying a Ruger bolt action .308 with Leupold scope from the man he had anonymously turned in. The guy needed the quick cash to pay his fine.

Buddy still smiled when he thought about that sucker! Buddy knew he was capable of much worse. Knew, in fact, he had done much worse on more than one occasion.

Scott was a fine shot; quick with a knife. Buddy had even begun training him to quickly cape a game head. He and Ronnie were his best movers of heroin into the local communities, as well as best suppliers of deer hair. With a call for bear parts and organs as well as portions of elk on the rise, Buddy had considered using Scott to expand his inventory. But the boy had begun coming apart at the seams the last couple of evenings. Showing up late, often past midnight. Wanting "to talk." Referencing woman troubles.

Had even told Buddy that he was perhaps his "best friend." Blurred lines. Erratic behavior. Maybe it was time to promote Ronnie.

Ronnie was quieter, more controlled; but very ambitious. Ronnie would do what needed done. Scott had become a liability. Buddy did not like liabilities, and like the much younger and impressionable Ronnie—did what had to be done.

Chapter Eleven

Scott arrived at the bridge just before sundown; watched the creek wind its way beside a bluff and along a field as it entered the four eighteen-inch culverts beneath the concrete passage. Watched it meander out of sight on its way to adding its spring-fed flow to the river. Had taken the evening off from the job with his uncle. Remembered well the brief conversation.

"What's the big deal?" he had replied when the uncle seemed a bit perturbed at his asking off for the evening. "Not like we have anybody on the books for the weekend."

"We have maintenance work to do. Work for which I pay you and expect done!" had countered the uncle. "I suspect another evening spent with delinquents? I'm not sure why my brother doesn't seem to care; but that's my family name as well that you've been dragging through the muck. You were raised better than that. If not by word, at least by example. Your father and mother are honest people. I am honest. Why do you hang around with thieves?"

Scott had left midsentence. Sure, they were honest people. And what did it get them? Working six and seven days a week. Old homes and used cars; bad backs and empty wallets. Nothing like the cash Buddy flashed around. He had swung by the tackle shop, told Buddy where he was headed. Buddy had not asked why, just gave him a six pack "on account." A perk Scott enjoyed often.

"On account we're partners" he'd laughingly called back as he grabbed the cold beverages and headed for his private rendezvous. Figured he had perhaps a couple of hours before this meeting he somewhat dreaded. Time to drink a couple of beers while collecting his own thoughts and deciding just what all he should say and how best to say it. Was on his second when he heard the crunch of gravel behind him.

Though surprised that Ronnie had arrived this early, figuring his friend to have other things to do and knowing he pretty well kept his own hours; he decided to not act alarmed. Not even bothering to turn around as he listened to the opening and closing of the truck door and the footsteps coming toward him, he casually asked over his shoulder, "You want a cold one?"

His answer was the sudden protrusion of an arrow from out his shirt pocket. Or more accurately, the hunting tip and first three inches of an arrow through his shirt pocket; for it had entered his body from the back. There was still enough light for Scott to see the blood covered razor-edged blades---all three. He could make out the *Muzzy 100* on the broadhead. This was his final thought as massive blood loss caused his heart to stop and him to fall to the ground. Mercifully he would not feel the weapon pulled on out the front of his torso by a gloved hand. His cold fingers somehow still gripped the half empty aluminum can when later he was found.

Chapter Twelve

"Look what a hole!" was the excited comment Mark heard
as he neared the scene in his beloved park. Two county deputies
were staring at what appeared to be a young male covered in blood.

"What kind of gun did this, you think?" was the inquisitive offering
of the second.

"State boys will figure it out" stated the sheriff as he exited
his vehicle, having arrived within seconds of the Park Ranger Mark
Williams.

"Morning, boys," greeted Mark as he walked on up to the
scene. "Morning, Sheriff. Thanks for the call."

"Procedure," was the Sheriff's somewhat curt reply. He was
re-elected every four years pretty much on an anti-Federal
government platform. "We got the State boys coming in for the
crime scene unless you want to try and take this off our hands."

"No, just want to be involved; kept up to speed" Mark
responded. "ID the body yet?" Though within feet of the young
man, as he was now turned facedown, Mark had no idea at whom he
was looking.

"Scott Haden" was the subdued response. Mark reached out
to steady himself on the nearby truck; caught himself realizing the

last thing needed was another set of fingerprints to clear from the scene. Taking a breath, he spoke.

"Who found the body?" hoping the depersonalization would help him deal with the flood of images and thoughts crashing into his mind. A father rising immediately to the defense of his son. A boy laying down a beautiful sacrifice bunt to advance his team in last year's district playoffs. Sacrifice? Is that what this was about? A life sacrificed to destroy any path to the answers sought in a murder?

"Anonymous tip" replied the sheriff. "Came in late last night. Clerk thought it was a prank. 'Body by a bridge.' Have any idea how many bridges in this county? Started checking them at daylight. Arriving any earlier wouldn't have helped. Haven't contacted the family yet. Thought I'd head out there now. We'll keep you posted."

Mark was somewhat relieved he was not invited to ride along. He wished to keep his communication with the father confidential; and also dreaded the father's response. Would he now blame him—Mark—and his investigation for the death of his son? Was he somehow to blame? He needed someone with whom to talk. To share concerns and generate ideas; to divine the path to truth that would put an end to these heinous acts. But whom? No one he could think of in the Corps or the sheriff's office, though both departments certainly held some quite competent personnel.

The sheriff himself was nobody's fool; just not interested in making waves in a campaign season. And with elections every four years, he considered everyday campaign season. Poaching, marijuana; even meth did not bother him much. The first he saw simply as redneck sport; the latter two crimes of little consequence. Not that he considered drugs a victimless crime; he just considered the victims mostly volunteers. He believed and was heard to comment more than once "Nobody forces them to take the stuff!" Joe Barnes was a Baptist, born and bred. And like many in his congregation, despised demon alcohol each Wednesday and Sunday but was likely to drink a cold beer on a Friday or Saturday evening. Especially if alone.

Murder was different; hence the call to bring in the state forensics team. First, a government biologist; now a high school kid. Joe Barnes would not tolerate such goings on in his county. And in the days to come all within earshot would hear such affirmations. Ranger Williams just was not sure behind the bluster and bluff how deep of a skill set really existed.

The Conservation Corps had its own law enforcement in the form of Game Wardens. Some good honorable and hardworking men. Mark's concern here was that if they could or would not stop the rampant poaching in the county, he could not help but wonder what chance they had at this. It was the strong belief of not only Mark, but a good deal of the farmers who were constantly finding dead deer in their roadside fields that staking out and following a handful of suspects could have brought the poaching to a stop long before.

Mark continued to ponder his next move as he exited the scene. Normally a man comfortable to keep his own counsel, he felt this was beyond him. Walking back to the truck after taking pictures and notes for his own records, for this crime was in his jurisdiction; he thought back to the one deputy's question. What gun did make such a hole? Reaching the privacy of his own vehicle, he closed his eyes for a moment.

Anyone watching may have easily assumed he was catching a moment of rest. In fact, it was much more. For though he was still unsure of what earthly counsel upon which he should prevail; he had no doubt to whom he should direct his petition for wisdom and strength, as well as for solace for the family of this latest victim. Mark was in prayer with his Heavenly Father.

Chapter Thirteen

The crime was on the radio by noon; the television news later that evening. This was the second murder in less than a week in a community that had not had a single murder in almost three decades. Forensics had been completed, but nothing was being released to the public. I was at a loss as to what was happening in the sleepy little place I call home. We had crime, but welfare had taken care of most petty theft and methamphetamine cookers were being put out of business by the cheap supply of heroine coming into the country. Like much of rural America, we looked fairly calm on the surface.

That is until now. All the ugliness that comes with the mortality of mankind had been brought to the surface by these recent acts. The selfish and unkind deeds; the criminal and common were now exposed as public knowledge served as rays of sunlight to secrets best surviving in the dark. Unlike the one child of Dicken's Spirit of Christmas Present; it had not been ignorance that kept such fare from everyday conversation. It had been the apathy that too often drains the marrow from otherwise steeled backs.

I remember, I believe, that apathy was one of those foes with which Rostand's *Cyrano* fought with at the end. I know for sure it was what Horace Greeley called "living oblivion." It was the downhill slide of many a business; the coming demise of present society. When not able to find my solitude in the woods, I often found a sense of peace and wisdom when devouring the words of great writers from earlier times and different places.

I thought back now to words read and remembered from many years past. I searched for something that would remind me of the humanity that though on occasions might seem overwhelmed but is present in all stories of man; for guidance as to how these murders could be solved. Surely Doyle and Poe had encountered and conquered more brilliant foes; Camus overcome more lethargic times.

I had run, not jogged, a good five miles this evening after leaving the office. Had done so in the company of Rex and with a bottle of water on my left hip and my Ruger LCP on my right. I had moved it from its normal ankle holster to a paddle holster for the run. Though on a county road that neared the edge of the river, and admittedly a bit anxious about our recent crimes, the .380 automatic was not a new addition to my apparel. It pretty much went wherever I did; had since its purchase seven years ago. A girl can't be too careful.

Dinner was grilled chicken and asparagus. I kept a small gas grill on the back porch of my apartment; enjoyed the contrast of cooking outdoors in the cold. Now I was actually drawing a "plot board" above my desk. This was usually what I used to outline an article or one of my more complex legal briefs. Now it was how I was trying to solve two murders.

At the top was the elk; not placed by priority, but by timeline. I then had two columns. Middleton heading one; the Haden kid at the top of the other. A broken line with a question mark connected the two. In parenthesis, I had recorded the dates and approximate times, though this latter entry had windows of several hours for each victim----human and otherwise. So far, that was about it. I started a third column; possible suspects.

This last was developing quite vague. Farmers that did not want the repatriation; no specifics. Black market for elk parts. Weak, because currently elk lips were bringing more than antlers if the internet could be believed. Kids poaching. Hard to believe this would lead to murder. This last group bothered me, as I had trouble comprehending children raised in rural America would have such disrespect for game and also had a hard time understanding why more was not done to stop it. If you stopped five people in our town and asked who was involved, at least four could give you their names.

Not necessarily would, mind you; but could. And one of those names would have been Scott Haden. This from the girl that weekly does my nails. A long time ago I learned to not ask, just sit and listen. Salons, cafes and repair shops. The occasional checkout line at the grocery. Unfortunately, some of the least reliable are the different media, especially governmental press releases.

What had rarely been spoken of was now everyday conversation. I intended to keep listening. One ripple on the now no longer calm veneer would eventually become a wave, and I hoped that I would be one of the first to hear it!

Chapter Fourteen

Jim Skaggs had been with the Conservation Corps for more than a decade. The last five years had been as a subordinate to James Middleton and assisting with the repatriation of the elk into the river region of the southcentral Ozarks. With a degree in Infectious Disease, it had been his assignment to monitor the health of the herd as it was grown. He inspected each animal prior to release; continued the monitoring through animal spoor and the occasional drugging of individual animals with dart guns.

For more than a year, he had been studying the possible causes of Chronic Wasting Disease (CWD) spreading in elk; paying particular attention to the single protein prions that attached themselves to grasses and he believed enabled the disease to remain in soil and then be spread as grasses grew and were eaten. He had done work in this area going back decades, including helping to identify the fact that high potassium levels in soil had as much to do with grass tetany as the low magnesium levels associated with early spring growth. He had been part of the study that identified bird's foot trefoil as an alternate legume to alfalfa to prevent bloat in cattle.

In recent years, he had concentrated on *zoonotic* diseases; those that could transfer between animal and human populations--- such as anthrax. The *Black Bane* of the 17th century had wiped out more than 60,000 head of cattle in Europe, creating an economic disaster. Though there was no evidence at present that CWD was such a disease, the fact that the proteins involved were impervious to the normal kill strategies of extreme heat and ultraviolet light had worried him for some time. It was this area that had led to the majority of he and Middleton's rather heated arguments.

He believed cattle farmers in the release zone had very legitimate concerns, as did those sportsmen that already valued the trophy white-tailed deer hunting of the area. The smaller cousins were definitely at risk of CWD from any elk population. Jim believed it only a matter of time before CWD became zoonotic and that local human populations were at risk as well.

Recent legislation moved the state's "fenced" deer herd from under the jurisdiction of the Corps to the state's agricultural department. Cooperation between the two agencies could be better, at least Jim believed; and his frustration grew at the Corps' inability to get more specific data about the numbers of incidents, not that the Corps was very forthcoming in sharing their own data either. He did know that at least in the wild population, CWD was spreading.

He also knew that there had been at least two deaths of mature bulls that had been necropsied at their state office and that he had yet to see either report. Now, with Middleton's death, he was at what appeared to be a dead end. Records were either lost or had been misplaced; the animals' carcasses now destroyed. Fellow staff would not talk about either incident.

Almost none of this had he shared with Mark Williams earlier that afternoon, save for the background of CWD and his job description with the Corps. Certainly, nothing about the extra deaths or the rumors of illegal activity. The Park Ranger was known to be a man who could be trusted; still Jim had not divulged much. Basically, had answered enough questions to be polite.

A lot was riding on this project, for both the state agency and the private foundations working closely with them. A lot was riding on this for Jim, as well. Two large out of state ranches had already proffered job opportunities based on his success. A success that was rapidly disappearing.

Chapter Fifteen

Sheriff Barnes was tired. Physically, and if there was such a thing, politically. He'd been elected for the fourth time a little over three years ago, needed one more term to carry him into retirement. Already there was talk of one of his own deputies running against him. Calling off a search for some lost hikers two years ago had come quickly back to bite him in the behind. The local coroner had been extremely outspoken with his opinions, which included his belief that while the deputies and sheriff were lying in their warm beds, a man and his nephew had been freezing to death. He swore "they were still breathing an hour before they were found."

Barnes had believed them hopelessly lost and "impossible to find." They were located along an often-traveled log road not fifteen minutes from town. That and a meth lab fire killing a couple of young kids had left him vulnerable to a challenge. This elk debacle along with two murders had him chasing his tail. He couldn't even blame the Feds, as locals had been given jurisdiction.

State lab boys had helped some. The Corps fellow, Middleton, had been shot and dumped in the Current River and then floated up on a gravel bar downstream. Small caliber handgun at close range. Nine millimeter or possibly a .380; not sure as the bullet had fragmented so greatly. The kid was killed with a bow and arrow, at least according to "the experts." Nothing had been found in the Haden corpse either, but forensics detailed

"cuts made by razor sharp blades spiraling through the body."

He had nothing. Supposedly the boy was part of the group that had been spotlighting. Who didn't know that? He had always considered that a fairly victimless crime; did a bit himself prior to being elected High Sheriff of the county. Game violations were a Corps' matter, and even they knew no local judge or prosecutor was going to go out on a political limb for a hundred dollar fine.

Insurance companies all agreed that there were far too many deer and constantly lobbied the Commission for more liberal limits on the harvest. Numerous farmers considered deer a nuisance, giving them the moniker "government billy goats" in derision to their support. And elk? Just free roaming "cows" waiting to be hit by cars or to crowd down fences just in time to

ruin someone's hay harvest.

The murders, well those were troublesome. The only killings up to now were done in the heat of passion at one of the few remaining roadhouses or at someone's home. Generally, the "perp" was nearby or even still at the scene. These killings were now going on their second week with no real leads. Still no similarities or connections between the two victims.

No visible motives. Neither person had been robbed. No real evidence to indicate that either person might have known their assailant. The high schooler had been shot in the back, the arrow not yet found. The biologist had been shot in the side, the bullet fragmenting on the ribs before entering the lungs and heart. No way to tell if he had seen someone approaching him either.

One had been killed where found; the other at a point upstream. Blood at the scenes indicated as much. Neither had been armed. Neither was known to have had any enemies. Sheriff Barnes was near a crossroad. Let the state boys find more evidence? Begin to chase down rumors? Roust the usual suspects? And if so, who in tarnation were the usual suspects?

Chapter Sixteen

"You know I hate to put you in this situation, but I have to ask" Mark Williams told the gentleman seated before him. He had driven almost three hours to catch the young man far away from their home community. Previous encounters had led to his knowledge that the Corps' employee had an elderly grandmother in a nursing home in a neighboring city. It was here that Mark had driven to and waited.

"I can't believe you would bother me here" the man said angrily. "This isn't right."

"First, I did not 'bother' you during your visit. I got your attention and asked you to share a cup of coffee after you had visited your grandmother. Second. What is 'not right' is the fact that we have had two murders inside of a month and we—the law—have gotten nowhere." Mark's response was measured, but equally emotional. "Now, who else knew about the peripheral concerns at the Corps?"

"I'm not sure I know what you mean" the younger man replied.

"For one thing, Middleton's assistant has a degree in infectious disease. His work is cited all over the internet. And he's assigned to less than one hundred and fifty animals here in the

Ozarks. What gives?" Mark had prepared himself well for this interview.

"There are some concerns about CWD. That wasting disease. You know...."

"I know about Chronic Wasting Disease. I have my own cattle herd, and my own concerns. Go on. What is the public not being told?"

"Well, Middleton's assistant and Middleton were seen arguing a lot. Seems there were rumors of the elk being infected. That we, the Corps, had actually put some animals down and had them taken for necropsies at the state office. Skaggs had been left out of the information loop. There were also rumors that we, again the Corps, had been harvesting and selling semen. Illegally. Nothing sanctioned, but a couple of the tech assistants with access to dart guns and electrical stimulus equipment."

Mark was keenly aware of how animals were sedated and semen harvested for artificial insemination. The process was common among high cost registered livestock.

"Why these elk?" Mark inquired.

"Because somehow we got some unbelievable genetics in the first release. Of seven bulls, five were royals; you know genuine six by six racks. One was an 'Imperial' with seven large tines on each side. At three years-old, another was headed to be but was killed in an accident of some kind. Something happened while he was sedated. That is statistically far beyond average.

Private breeders would pay a fortune for such a specimen. Couldn't very well sneak a half-ton bull out of the park, but could secretly get the semen."

Mark sat there, both surprised and appalled by the audacity of such an in-house operation.

"Do you think either is true? Are they infected? Could someone be selling semen? What you say is for me only. I need somewhere to start."

"I really can't help you. I've told you what little I know; what more I have heard. The state office is worried about something. There are calls all the time transferred back to offices where conversations cannot be overheard. There were the arguments of which I've told you. I can only add, I hope in the strictest of confidence, what I think. We did have requisitions for equipment and vehicles that had no authorization from where it should have come. I think something big is up. My guess would be the herd is all infected and that the Corps is trying to cover it up, including to the point of floating the story about black market semen sales."

Mark took another drink of his coffee. If rumors of illegal sales were true, he knew where to look. What he did not know was how.

"Thanks!" he told the young man as they parted at the cafeteria door. "And I wish you to know, I keep your grandmother in my prayers. As I do you." With that, Mark walked to his own vehicle and to his own thoughts as he began the long drive back to his home.

Chapter Seventeen

My father had taught me to fly fish. "If you wait long enough" he would say "you will hear the water talk to you. Telling you where to cast." He was gone now, victim of mesothelioma. Died of cancer at forty-eight; never having smoked a day in his life. Years spent during his youth in a Navy shipyard. But his teachings remained, as did the similar words of Izaak Walton and Ernest Hemingway.

I was unsure if water really talked, but I could hear again my father's voice when alone on a quiet stretch of water. I was also sure that if you listened long and hard enough anywhere, you would hear things. Eventually, important things. Just this past week I had finally done so.

I now had a connection between the victims. The two human victims, at least. Scott Hayden had a girlfriend, albeit in recent months an on-again off-again sort of thing. A very pretty and ambitious girl. A vey worldly girl. A miss Molly Roberts. Cheerleader. Conservation corps volunteer. And most recently the vivacious shadow attached to Corps biologist and elk expert James Middleton as his seemingly infatuated assistant.

Although a licensed attorney in this and three other states, my only visits to the courtroom were to provide information to the lawyer leading a case; my only appearances before a jury as an expert witness, and this generally dealing with numbers and their manipulation. I had on numerous occasions been the person that had organized a winning assault or defense, depending on which was the present client's needs.

I was a whiz with charts and graphs and it was to that end I now applied my energies. Tax season was about to become hundred hour weeks at least for the next three months, so I very much wished to solve these cases now. A second bedroom that I had converted to a study was now papered in such machinations. What had started out as a single poster with a trio of columns was now taking up the better part of an entire wall. Beloved framed photographs had been either relocated to other rooms or carefully wrapped in bath towels and stacked in a closet. Curtains pulled completely so that more wall space was available.

Catching fish is about far more than just knowing where to cast. What to cast is equally important. I now had direction; I needed more. I knew who to ask; still did not have the what. In putting together flow charts, as with algebraic equations, the emphasis was largely on how each entry affected the next.

I now knew that both victims shared a common denominator; friendship with the same person. Sooner or later one can find a relationship of some kind between almost anyone, even if you have to become so generic as they lived in the same state at the same time. But this was more. The dating relationship with Miss

Roberts was no surprise for Scott Haden; they were, after all, classmates.

The relationship between Dr. Middleton and her was a bit different, at least on the surface. A simple case of mentoring. Innocent enough; there had been such relationships in my own past. I clerked for a man my father's age when in law school; had assisted a professor as an undergraduate to defer tuition. In fact, most of my relationships educationally and professionally were with older men. Middleton and Roberts was probably at worst a young girl's minor infatuation and an older man's appreciation of the attraction of youth.

I decided to make a list of possible benefits and detriments. In general, I had first asked myself who might gain from the crimes, beginning with the elk killing and mutilation. A poacher for bragging rights. With the first murder, the same. I wondered if it might not be the same man, worried that the Corps biologist had information that might lead to the poacher's identification and arrest.

With the second murder, third crime; I again pondered possible beneficiaries of the high school student's death. A rival on the baseball team as district play would begin in a few months and college scholarships would be on the line. Not likely, even though the Haden boy was a good player and would be one of the first to catch any college scout's eye. A rival for the girl. Again, doubtful as at this level break-ups were much more common than murder. Besides, the relationship was off as often lately as it was on.

I had heard the rumors about the poaching; knew some of the farmers that had found carcasses left to rot. Had even heard a few of the names, one of which was his. There I drew another line, as now there was a possible connection between the first and third of the crimes. Had Scott been involved in the killing of the elk and later silenced for his knowledge? Another line drawn, as I now had another connection. Had Middleton been about to pressure Scott into talking and the murderer just killed out of sequence; opportunity establishing the timeline and chain of events, not necessarily priority of risk?

Back to Miss Roberts. What to ask her when I went to see her; a decision I had unconsciously made an hour ago. "What did I need to solve this?" I wondered. For starters, somehow I need to respectfully ascertain how each death had affected her life. Benefits and detriments.

I called a counselor at the local school with whom I'd worked a couple of river clean-ups. I had spoken with several students at one of these, a club there to acquire community service hours needed for membership requirements. Molly Roberts had been among those students. She agreed to set up a meeting at the end of school; my concern for her loss the cover.

I went over my upcoming interview in my head. How had each death possibly made her life better? And, sadly, how had they made her life worse? The answer to the latter seemed obvious. Death of a boyfriend; loss of a mentor.

Realizing Molly Roberts was in no way a suspect herself, and had just suffered two personal losses back to back, I was rethinking my desire to meet with her as she entered the office and took a seat. The young lady before me looked older; less vivacious. Loss will do that to you.

Noticing the bandage on her right hand, I asked "Does it hurt?"

"Which? These cuts or the two funerals I've attended in less than as many weeks?"

"I meant, I guess, the cuts. I saw the bandage was all. I am sure the passing of friends hurts much more." I no longer wanted to ask her anything. After all, one question was already answered and the other---"What did you gain by the violent deaths of two humans?"—well, I could think of no good way to ask. Perhaps I was not yet done listening to the water.

Chapter Eighteen

Buddy was mad and getting madder by the minute. The nerve of some people. Public servants that worked for him. He paid taxes, at least on part of his earnings. A long day had got suddenly worse when he watched not one but two law dogs pull into his driveway. This was nothing like the visit the day after the elk was found mutilated and Dr. Middleton came by and left his card; requesting that if the local business owner heard anything he would appreciate a call. No, this was much different.

The good Sheriff Barnes himself had barely shut off his Tahoe when Park Ranger Mark Williams pulled in beside him. The sheriff had done most of the speaking, asking if they could come in and then wanting to know if "he'd heard anything." Like he was some kind of stool pigeon.

He had cooperated, for a number of reasons; not least of which they had badges. Badges but no search warrant. Yet. With two trophy heads in his freezer out back, the last thing he wanted was the law with search warrants.

"Had he known either victim? What was their relationship? Mind if we look around?" To the last he had politely said no, he had too many "projects" for other people he did not wish to disturb; knowing full well they would be back later with that much-dreaded piece of paper. To the first two, he talked.

Like any good liar, and he considered himself one of the best, Buddy knew to include as much of the truth as possible. Sure, he knew them both. Middleton sometimes fished the lake; he believed he had on occasion sold him bait and maybe even a few hooks and such. Had seen him briefly sometime last week. Buddy knew to never offer specifics. After all, if a president could have a poor "ready recollection", why not a simple bait shop owner.

The boy? He dropped by from time to time with some friends. "Out of high school a couple of years, I think. Played a little ball in his day." Buddy offered these tidbits to cover any proof they might offer later of he having given the boy beer. "Honest mistake; thought he was older" would be his response if that became necessary.

"Dropped by one day last week late" again in case the law knew more that they were letting on. "Seemed pretty troubled about something. Some kind of falling out with a friend. Maybe woman trouble!" Let them harass the Roberts girl for a while.

"There was a time I did business with the boy. Bought deer hair from him and some of his friends. Always assumed it was legal; bow season running most of the fall." This latter was when the ranger asked about the Haden kid's possible involvement in area poaching. "Maybe even bought some this past year. I'd have to check my records and see. Mind you I'm not the best bookkeeper around." He delivered this line with a smile. Both officers saw it as a smirk.

Buddy had begun to get angry when the ranger had informed him they would be back. Not that the threat surprised him, it was just that the message was delivered as just that. A threat! The sheriff piled on.

"We know about the drugs. The poaching. I've got two murders to solve, and I'm going to solve them. If we have to camp out here and question everybody that comes through that door for the next month, so be it. Stevens, you've brought this on yourself. Life as you knew it has ended. I'll lighten up when I see someone behind bars!"

With that the two had left. Buddy was furious----and just a bit scared. He knew he did not have much time to get rid of the freezer's contents. He knew the deer heads were the least of his problem, though neither had an accompanying tag. Both had been shot in the dead of night. To both acts there had been a witness; at least he was gone. Now to tie up some more loose ends.

Chapter Nineteen

Jim Skaggs did not believe in coincidences. Never had.
This evening was the second time he'd been interviewed in as many
days. First the ranger, now this burnout of a reporter. A has been
looking for one more "good" headline. Jim figured the guy was
hoping for better things, fairly sure that part time reporting could
not pay much for a paper the size of the local weekly. With a
readership counted in the hundreds, Skaggs surmised that a really
good story might land this old guy a better job on a larger paper.
Burnout or not, the guy had some good questions. First about elk
diseases and how they might be transmitted. He had told him much
the same he had told Williams. Then the ex-Seal had surprised him.
Wanted to know about how they sedated the elk and why.

"How would the animal act after being hit with a dart?" he
had inquired. Wanted specifics. "Would its gait have changed?
How far could it travel?" The questions had gone on for half an
hour.

Skaggs had answered what he could; became more hesitant
when the reporter began to ask him to speculate, even guess.
Sharing some insight with a fellow governmental employee such as
the ranger was one thing, and Mark Williams did have the
reputation of being honest. Speaking to a member of the media was
another, especially one with alcohol on his breath.

68

"You looking for backstory on the elk killing, or something more?" Skaggs had finally asked the reporter.

"Just something to sell" was the response. "Just something to sell!"

After another hour of more conversation than interrogation, the reporter had left. Thanked Jim for his time, even offered a "hit" from the flask in his coat pocket. A gesture Jim declined. Jim ate a late supper. Did get a cold beer from the refrigerator and gave it all some thought. The elk; Dr. Middleton and the kid. This much crime in what had been a fairly peaceful town in such a short time seemed almost assuredly related. An elk and an elk expert killed within days and within the same mile of riverfront.

He thought of the unauthorized equipment use; the unaccounted-for tranquilizer darts and the focus of much of the reporter's questioning. Still could not figure why Middleton was killed, and what he had been doing at the river in the first place. His desire to leave the Corps and go to work on a private ranch was increasing; his opportunities he feared were headed the opposite direction. Tomorrow he would call one of his contacts at the Arizona game ranch. He had several questions he needed answers to; whether or not he left the Corps. Like how bad was CWD on private game ranches and how valuable was semen from an outstanding herd bull.

Chapter Twenty

Mark had agreed to stay behind. Parked about a half-mile down the highway, he would be able to see any vehicles coming from or going to the bait shop. Sheriff Barnes had made the suggestion, in part due to the fact that Ranger Williams' truck did not have the large insignia let alone light bar as did his Tahoe. He had promised to have a deputy out there in less than an hour in an unmarked car of their own to continue the observation throughout the night.

Both lawmen agreed that Stevens was hiding something, and now the sheriff had finally had his fill of what had been a cancer on the mostly legitimate businesses of the county for far too long. The two murders were the proverbial straws on the camel's back. Barnes was apoplectic at the thought these crimes might somehow remain unsolved, and well aware that each day that passed with no new leads increased that possibility.

Mark thought of what he knew. The elk herd might be infected; probably was, at least to some degree. A full-blown epidemic would be disastrous. Not only an imminent danger to surrounding cattle herds, but to the whitetail population and a multi-million-dollar hunting industry in the state. A terrible blow to the Corps. If what he had learned about the soil retention of disease was correct, this would have an impact on the over seventy-five thousand acres of public land that made up the park as well.

It might mean the putting down of more than a hundred animals; a possible death knell for the repatriation of elk in the Missouri Ozarks. The declaration of private farms as toxic for cattle grazing. Litigation could be immense.

Then there were the murders. Somewhere in the community he called home was a killer; possibly two, and the law no closer to catching them. In the lighted structure they had just left were answers. His thoughts were on what they might find if tomorrow they could obtain a search warrant. He stayed alert knowing that any vehicle movement might well be an attempt to dispose of such evidence; hence the stakeout. At least any and all trips could be monitored and possibly multiple warrants attained as needed.

It was in this state of intent scrutiny that he clearly saw the flames erupt into the night and leap skyward. Though he was there within little more than a minute, starting his pickup while radioing the sheriff's department and hurriedly driving as fast as safety allowed, the shed in the back of the store complex was completely engulfed when he arrived. Exiting his vehicle with flashlight in hand, he ran to see if lives were in danger.

"Hold up there, partner" he was hailed as he approached the fire. Heat had already put up an all but invisible wall that may have stopped him if the voice had not. "No one's inside. Just those projects I told you boys about earlier. Some engine parts and cleaning supplies." Buddy looked a bit dirty but no worse for wear from this catastrophe.

"I was afraid you guys might bump into something and get dirty ----or worse" the owner continued. "Well, I think I accidentally kicked over a space heater while trying to straighten the place up. I got out okay, but I'm afraid the building's a goner. Good thing I've got insurance."

As they had been talking, a deputy arrived and then shortly afterwards the first of two firetrucks; a substation not quite three miles away. By then the structure was falling in on itself. One of the trucks used its tank to spray the wall of the store that was facing the fire, the crew chief on hand recognizing the shed was a complete loss. In only ten more minutes the sheriff and another deputy had arrived.

"You thinking what I'm thinking?" Mark confided to Sheriff Barnes after he walked over, sure to keep his voice low so as to not be overheard.

"Should have brought marshmallows?" was all Joe said. He wore the half-smile of a man too old to cry and too tired to outright laugh. After checking with the fire chief and speaking to his deputies, he nodded towards Mark and left for home. Mark went over and thanked the deputies and firefighters for their quick response; got into his truck to do likewise.

"Guess I should have let you guys look around when you were here earlier." Buddy had silently followed Mark to his vehicle, had begun speaking as Mark was about to close the driver's door. "Feel free to come back tomorrow, though. The ashes should be cool by evening." This time Mark was sure the face before him displayed a smirk, not a smile. And did so by design.

Chapter Twenty-One

Ronnie had been pretty much keeping to himself since that night. He still could see his friend lying there with the blood all over the gravel bar on which he lay. Despite the road that had led to this and the part he himself had played, he could not stand the thought of his former teammate being eaten on by scavengers as had happened to the corpse of the biologist, Middleton. Hence the anonymous call.

He had not remained long at the sight; sickened by what had transpired and anxious about being caught at the scene. He thought back to his conversations with Buddy and the eventual involving of Scott in their illegal affairs. Suspected that Scott was involved in even worse activities than the poaching contests. Thought of his last conversation with Buddy that had taken place what seemed an eternity ago but could be measured in hours.

Ronnie had been drinking more heavily; had stayed away from school as well as from the majority of his acquaintances. He did not wish to see or hear Buddy; perhaps never again. Their relationship had come with too much of a price. What good was the extra cash now that he no longer had his friend with whom to spend it?

Never one to pay attention in church, and not even one to attend now that his parents no longer made him; still, teachings from the past had him considering Heaven and Hell. Leaving Scott that evening; revisiting the bloody scene over and over in his mind-- all made him reconsider the consequences of his actions.

All of them.

With little success, he had tried to think of the good times. The simultaneous stolen bases; the many successful hit and runs. Scott had been fearless on the base paths, always confident that Ronnie had had his back.

"You're my man!" Scott had exclaimed one afternoon when on the second occasion Ronnie had leaned far out of the batter's box to put the ball in play on a called pitch out, knowing Scott was already well on his way to the next base. "You're always there for me," he had said.

Always there for myself, Ronnie could not help but think. For myself. He had finally called up Molly one evening, believing in shared misery, he could find some sense of solace. He was wrong. The get-together had gone poorly. He had drunk too much; made the conversation too much about himself and what he was going through. Too little about her, and she with the loss of the same friend. He realized that after she had gone and he had begun to sober up.

He wondered what to do now? The law seemed to still be clueless about all three crimes. He himself had limited knowledge of two. The one he kept trying to put out of his mind.

Ronnie decided to go back to school this coming week. Though baseball season and even practice were weeks away, he had to keep his grades up. Now maybe he should put more time into a sport that had always come fairly easily. Work on his slider and breaking ball. Hit the weights and see if he couldn't get a bit more heft into his swing. Colleges liked a good hitting pitcher.

Chapter Twenty-Two

Jim Skaggs was at a loss. The friend from out west had finally returned his call. A private ranch had been forced to destroy more than a hundred animals. Mule deer and mostly elk. Shoved their carcasses off into a newly dug trench; burned and buried them. Converted nearly ten sections of land to grass and pheasant hunting; unsure of when it would again be safe graze for either of their antlered offerings. A blow that nearly caused a well-funded and quite large operation to go under. All because of CWD testing positive in both the animals and the grass.

What he learned next was even more interesting. Seems all that kept them from bankruptcy was the herd they were building up on their remaining land; a still impressive twelve thousand acres. They had purchased some elk semen and artificially inseminated a dozen of their best cows. This was five years ago. These elk now were huge, with heavy bodies and all of the male offspring with racks scoring in the 360-375 point range. Beginning three years ago, they had begun using these animals as herd bulls. Initially out of necessity; but now specifically for their genetics.

What got Jim's attention was the rumor that the semen had come from his elk project. One of his bulls. And even more disturbing was the rumor that the ranch was in the process of buying more of the same DNA from the same source. All quite under the radar and illegal as all get out. And somehow from his herd.

Jim was at a loss---what was he to do with this new information? Who had been involved and who had known? Was this what got Middleton killed?

The only sure elk crime he knew of was the recent mutilation of the large bull; but these criminals were after semen and not antlers. When he had asked what such semen might be worth, he was shocked. Could still not quite fully absorb the number he was given.

Not as quick to trust as the friend on the other end of the phone, he'd shared very few of his concerns. He had agreed that he should demand an immediate increase in the testing of the animals as well as the soils. He just wondered if behind his back this was not already being done. With Middleton gone and the state office saying nothing, Jim continued to wonder with whom he might be able to talk.

Chapter Twenty-Three

Molly rewrapped her hand; feeling glad that the stitches had now been removed. She could shower again without having to hold her hand outside the curtain or cover it with a plastic bag. She could move her fingers, and continued to be thankful that, though deep, the cuts had not affected ligaments or nerves. She'd been lucky.

She had stayed home the first week. Gone back to school the next, but took one more week off from cheerleading. Last night she'd rejoined the squad; district play now having begun. Still, she tempered her involvement and avoided any contact with fellow cheerleaders.

She missed Scott; much more that she believed possible. True, they had gone together for most of her Junior year; and like most of her friends, had been physically intimate. But it was over and she'd moved on. Or at least, so she had thought.

Of all things, her visit with Ronnie the other evening had better defined her sense of loss. Though Ronnie had done as usual and made the conversation about his problems and his loss; the majority of that loss was the absence of Scott from his life. The same absence she, herself, had been struggling to not feel. It was Ronnie's little anecdotes that had made this denial no longer possible.

Scott was always ready with a laugh, if even at his own expense. There were the thoughtful gestures. He had made her soup once and brought it over when she had the flu. Had helped her when a term paper was due; not that he was smarter, but he offered to do all the research and put in the library time during his study hall. She still remembered the color-coded index cards he had painstakingly assembled.

And the gifts. Flowers delivered to school, to her home. Even to her recent internship; a cause for more than one argument. She now remembered the possessiveness along with the jewelry and electronics. Always, there was the possessiveness. Especially since her summer job and the more recent evening class and internship. Then she remembered Dr. Middleton.

She began to miss James horribly, and, in doing so, her sadness for Scott turned again to anger. Who was he to believe he controlled her life? What was a boy's youthful adulation compared to a man's more weathered regard?

Her thoughts roamed then to another adult with whom she had spoken. Rachel Hunt. She thought of Ms. Hunt as an outdoor writer and conservationist, remembered their time briefly at a river clean-up. She was aware that Ms. Hunt worked at the courthouse or something; was frequently at least seen there. Something to do with taxes, she believed.

She had appreciated the professional taking the time the other day to check on her at school and ask about her feelings. She recalled that perhaps she had been a bit curt. Had even projected an anger that was becoming harder to maintain. Certainly, much more difficult to correctly direct.

She had had no reason to be angry at Ms. Hunt; no reason at all. She had far more reason to be angry with herself. And, of course, to be angry with Scott.

Chapter Twenty-Four

Ranger Mark Williams was continuing to assist with the sheriff's efforts to keep Buddy Stevens under constant surveillance. Even with Buddy's admission that he believed himself to blame for the fire, sticking with his original story that he'd most likely accidentally knocked over a space heater in a crowded and dirty workshop; Sheriff Barnes was able to convince the fire department of the chance of arson and so the scene was thoroughly investigated. Much to his dismay, nothing of consequence had been found.

In his spare time, for a ranger's duties here at the end of archery and gigging seasons had their own demands, Mark continued to look for clues to all three crimes. He still believed that in some way they might be connected. Some of them almost had to be.

He thought of the "purple passion sheets" he'd been given as an elementary student years ago; the duplicated worksheets that frequently held a series of items. Four objects; one of which you had to circle for "it did not belong." If these crimes were connected, or at least two of them were; then which "did not belong"?

The elk and the elk biologist were killed within one mile of each other. So Scott did not belong. Middleton and the high school boy were human, so the elk mutilation is out. Scott and the elk were most likely killed in the evening, so Middleton's out as he was killed at night. Middleton was shot with a pistol, the elk a rifle and the boy a bow. They're all out!

Buddy Stevens acknowledged relationships with both the biologist and the ballplayer. How can anyone know an elk, so the elk's out? This was becoming confusing! Mark knew, but could not prove, that Stevens sold illegal mounts and condoned and possibly encouraged the tail game as well as underage drinking by local kids. He "who would cause one of these little ones to sin."

Mark had no use for the man; would have proudly tied him to a millstone and have donated both rock and rope. Was Stevens at the center of all three crimes? It was with this belief that he was willing to give of his own free time to assist with the surveillance. He also hoped to do more. Somewhere was the key to these crimes and he continued to pray for the wisdom to find it as well as for peace for those families impacted by these horrific crimes.

Even outside his prayers, Mark thought of those affected. The man who perhaps too blindly had defended his son, but who now, would never again see him steal a base, turn a double play. Raise him grandchildren; cause him to laugh at some silly antic.

The teammates that had lost a friend. The cheerleader that had lost her boyfriend. The coach that lost, if not the leader, a good-natured "sparkplug" of frequent rallies.

The career biologist that would never marry. The Corps personnel that had lost a colleague. Mark even thought of the sheriff, who beside their differences, he knew to be a man of honorable intent. Joe Barnes wanted these murderers caught and punished. He might not get the biblical reference, but Joe would probably be all for that "drowned in the depths" solution as well.

Just like the arson investigation, another almost week had turned up nothing. In his briefcase were copies of not only the arson investigation, but of both autopsies and the necropsy. Tonight, he planned to once again read through all of them in depth. He was beginning to wonder if this crime was not beyond him. The criminal too smart; the confluences too confusing. While sitting again in the dark of a side road, Mark went once more to his Heavenly Father in prayer.

Chapter Twenty-Five

Buddy couldn't believe his good fortune. Everything he was worried about getting rid of had literally "gone up in smoke." Well, or smoldered in ashes. All the same, all evidence of criminal behavior was gone. Let them look long and hard, he knew he was in the clear.

He was even going to receive a several thousand-dollar insurance check for an old storage shed that had seen much better days. Seems the insurance carrier had not updated his policies for a while, and the only pictures they had on file showed a structure in a much better state of repair, and the contents they had covered included equipment sold off for cash years ago. Anyway he looked at it; this was a win-win for Mr. Buddy Stevens.

It was while in that celebratory mood that he answered the door. Seems the local paper was interested in doing a story, the structure lost being part of one of the first businesses servicing lake customers since the middle of the past century. The guy asking the questions and taking the pictures was some freelancer that wrote for several of the local papers at times. Buddy had recognized the name from a few bylines when he had handed him his card.

The reporter asked of the business's early days and Buddy related what he could from the stories told to him in his youth by parents and grandparents alike. Buddy declined to speak of the fire that had orphaned him somewhat early in his adulthood, choosing instead to recall the more pleasant of those vintage times.

The reporter moved to more specific questions about the loss and the fire itself. Had he been scared when the fire first erupted, that type of emotional line? He moved on to how the loss might affect his present level of services and then from here strayed into what all sorts of services did Buddy in fact offer tourists and returning clients. It was here Buddy felt a sense of déjà vu. He had been asked these questions before, in a somewhat different format. And he'd heard this voice before. Somewhere; sometime.

Chapter Twenty-Six

Rex and I had just finished watching an old *Andy Griffith* re-run. The one where we first meet the Darling Family. I think Rex liked the mountain music. I liked the idea of living in a town where the High Sheriff's biggest criminal dilemma was a miscreant rural family taking water for their truck from a trough meant for watering horses and then later slipping a few extra people into a hotel room that did not even have its own bath. Deputy Fife could likely handle that load.

I got up and went back to my study. Charts and index cards stared back as my dog and I perused the now somewhat cluttered walls. Somewhat cluttered, as all the materials were in neat rows and columns. Just not your regular decorative choices for an accountant slash conservationist recently turned rogue detective. I had used nice bright green twine to indicate connections. It kind of matched the forest green drapes; they chosen to accent the hardwood floors I had refinished myself. Spent a three-day weekend doing that. My mind was wandering!

I tried to focus. I was missing something. I had to be, but what? I needed more information. It was like I had a blueprint without specific measurements; or better yet, a spreadsheet with insufficient data. It was then my phone rang. The one in the kitchen that I did not carry. The land line.

"Hunt" I announced, saving the caller from having to deal with the antiseptic voice on the answering machine coldly announcing "Hunt residence. Leave a message." I believed myself much warmer in person.

"Miss Hunt? Rachel Hunt, the writer?" a male voice asked; one I believed I should recognize.

"In the flesh. Who's this and what can I do for you?"

Ten minutes later I hung up the phone. The conversation he desired was going to take some time. I had given him my address, no state secret, and invited him over. Now all I had to do was start some hot water for tea, find something we could snack on, and decide just how much I was going to tell and how far I believed I could trust this guy.

Chapter Twenty-Seven

Buddy continued to think about his present situation. The momentary euphoria of avoiding arrest diminishing; he now thought of his losses. He'd destroyed several thousand dollars-worth of trophy heads. He'd failed to deliver the product he'd promised to an out of state buyer. He'd lost a valuable asset and he knew he was being watched. He considered the resources he still had.

Buddy had acquired the assistance of the two part-time employees when they had approached him about possibly guiding on the lake. They didn't have much of a boat, weren't exceptional fisherman. What they were; was in need of extra funds and hoped to gain them without an extreme amount of physical effort.

Buddy's proposition had been simple. When they had droned on about the demeaning nature of their work, they had included the collection of semen for later artificial insemination. The two were surprised when he showed an interest in the process and were more than happy to describe in detail the steps of sedating mature elk with tranquilizer darts and then the use of electroejaculation to actually collect the semen from a large bull. Buddy put them to work.

Stevens had purchased semen a few years back from a similarly disgruntled employee; had not asked how it was acquired.

Figured now it had probably been originally obtained in a related fashion. When the original buyers had once again been contacted, he had found them ready and willing customers. A few extra equipment requisitions had worked their way through the system and he was in business. Until the shooter.

The very idiot that wanted to sell him some antlers, not even the complete head and skin cape that would make a much more valuable full shoulder mount possible, had ruined a fivefigure deal. The two ne'er do well workers had tracked the big bull with the imperial rack, as directed. Had made the shot and were stalking the animal until it dropped. As they approached with their equipment and cooler, they heard the shot. Saw someone in camo approaching the now felled bull and retreated. Went back to the four-wheeler parked only a few hundred yards away and called it a day.

Buddy had planned to have them target another of the large bulls, but with the killing of the biologist, had called the whole operation off. When he found out later that the shooter had ruined what should have been the first of several very profitable transactions, he was mad. He had refused to purchase the antlers anonymously; doing so for several reasons.

For one, the antlers by themselves would not bring that much money. Second, he wanted the Neanderthal that had ruined an operation he had been months in setting up. Figured the only way to identify him was to make the deal in person, "mano-a-mano."

How Buddy wished to get his hands on this idiot. But his insistence on anonymity had squelched any such chance. Still, Buddy knew he was missing something.

He did not wish to close the door on possible semen sales forever. His "state flunkies" were still ready to go; insisting they had learned from their mistakes. For one, they had gone out during the state's Alternative Season, almost assuring an increase in the number of hunters in the woods.

They also would increase the amount of sedative in the dart. They had originally decided to err on the side of a lower dosage, as any time an animal of such mass was put under, the chances of complications such as pneumonia increased the risks of their accidental death. Too much sedative could even cause immediate heart failure.

All these things were going through Buddy's mind as he opened another beer.

Chapter Twenty-Eight

Jim Skaggs had been more forthcoming than ever. Not only was any chance at a better career at stake, but so was his present job. If the herd would have to be destroyed, this job was most probably over. There had already been cutbacks in Corps offices around the state and his was an area where they might wish to make more. Even if not, any attachment to what appeared to be an environmental disaster would mar his profile and make him an easy candidate for replacement.

None of this was what he had shared with Mark. He had told him about the rampant spread of CWD in the Arizona ranch. He had told him some specifics about the local requisition of semen collection and storage equipment, though there was nothing in their current agenda for any such activities. He had also told him about the undocumented and unauthorized use of a Corps four-wheeler the day before the bull elk carcass was found on the park property.

This last was possible because of a Maintenance Request filed that next morning by a part-time worker. The worker claimed that when he went to get the vehicle that next morning it had damage to a rim, apparently from being run with a very low tire. The tire and tube were both ruined.

Mark was pondering this new information as he knocked on the apartment door before him.

"Come on in. I've got tea brewing" from the young lady who answered the door. "Would you like a cup?"

"Sure." Normally a coffee drinker, he wished to be polite. He knew Rachel Hunt by both reputation and several chance meetings over the years. He'd seen her at river clean-ups and a few times encountered her hiking in the forest. "Nothing added to it, though. Just brown or whatever color tea naturally is." With this last remark he felt somewhat foolish, aware of his level of discomfort now that he was here.

"Here" was what was obviously a second bedroom serving as a study and now a makeshift crime lab. Two walls were almost entirely covered by charts, photos and lists. Many of these were connected by what appeared to be green yarn. He took both the seat he was directed to and the cup and saucer being handed. A lifelong bachelor, he felt awkward in this tight of space with an attractive single woman this late at night. Of course, at six-foot five he often felt confined in normal ceilinged rooms and he reminded himself that this was a professional meeting.

"You think I'm nuts, right?" came the question from the almost petite figure before him. Rachel Hunt stood at most five and a half feet tall, nearly a full-foot shorter. She was athletic in build, and he noticed not for the first time the emerald eyes beneath hair the color of ripe persimmons. He was thinking about her smile when it finally dawned on him that there was a question on the table.

"No" he choked out, trying to soften what was naturally a loud voice. "Not at all. In fact, I'm thinking of remodeling my kitchen at home; might want the name of your decorator." He was old enough to be her father he reminded himself, and here on business.

"You've been busy. I appreciated the invite. I just got off the phone with Middleton's assistant; I guess former assistant. Let me bring you up to speed." The next two hours flew by. He told Rachel of Skaggs' revelations of possible illicit semen sales; all the time avoiding words like "electroejaculation" and "sperm." Mark told her what he had found in going through the autopsies and police reports. The accountant turned crime investigator took notes and occasionally asked for more specifics.

Mark told her of the comments handwritten on the bottom of the Haden boy's autopsy. The pathologist had noted that though it had not struck bone except for cutting through the edge of a rib and then exiting cleanly, tear wounds indicated that it had perhaps not passed completely through the body but had been pulled violently out. The location of fletching residue embedded in the exit wound did not match the trajectory the arrow had taken.

The examiner surmised that the shot had been taken from a great distance, that the arrow had lost velocity and had remained stuck in the body. The angle and other indications of needless trauma led them to believe it was pulled out by someone who hesitated; indicative of a first-time killer. As was the farther than effective distance from which the archer chose to shoot. All this Rachel was writing down.

"It's late. I need to go. Can we talk again soon?" Mark was tired, but glad to have someone with whom he could discuss not only the facts of the case but theories as well. As he bid her goodnight and turned for the door, he thought of the last thing Skaggs had told him. Decided it must be part of the equations and hypotheses they were developing.

"One last thing. Not sure I even want it written down. It's that thin and that potentially damaging." He took a breath; chose his words carefully.

"I knew James Middleton, not well but I knew him. Perhaps arrogant and aloof. Not unlike a lot of bureaucrat PhD's I've known over the years. His assistant said he had a 'thing' going with a local high school girl. Molly Roberts, a senior doing an internship in conjunction with a college class in which she was enrolled. Seems they had worked together most of the past summer when she volunteered with the Corps. Skaggs seemed to think there was something there. If we're going to work together, just thought you should know. I want to see these crimes solved. All of them. I don't want to see a good man's reputation unnecessarily tarnished in the process. Good night."

Mark had not intended to share that last part; had even cautioned Jim Skaggs about repeating such a thing to anyone else. It was just that he had become so comfortable with the young lady obviously equally passionate about the outdoors and as dedicated to solving these crimes. As he drove away, he thought of Ephesians 4:29; thought also of the Book of James. Silently raised a prayer that he had not just "set a great forest to blaze."

Chapter Twenty-Nine

I rinsed out the cups and saucers and put them in the dishwasher along with the dishes left over from a light supper; one fillet of tilapia and some brown rice, accompanied with a white wine and lemon sauce served over both some steamed asparagus and the fish. One plate, one frying pan and a small pot. After the later contributions from our work session, I added one of those little tablets and turned it on. Put the untouched cheese and grapes back in containers and in the refrigerator. I guess you don't support whatever that man must weigh on such light fare.

Not that Ranger Williams was fat, just big! We had spoken before, even hiked together for perhaps a mile one afternoon when we found ourselves on the same forest trail going the same direction. I had just never realized how tall and wide he was.

When he left, I almost stopped him. All evening I had been content to let him do most of the talking. I took notes that would soon become cards on the wall. That last revelation had been a bombshell. I had to admit I had wondered the same thing when seeing them at the river clean-up last summer. Once I thought I had caught Middleton staring at what was a very form-fitting T-shirt on what could be considered a voluptuous young body. But hey, I noticed.

Again, at the office that day, he had seemed "aloof." I thought her to be constantly near him; her choice or his was difficult to tell. When Mark, not Ranger Williams—was my little female mind wandering?—made the statement "if we're going to work together" and then entrusted me with information he was obviously uncomfortable sharing; I felt I should have been contributing more.

Like the tax records I had been uncovering about one possible suspect. I had accessed these records through a connection with another case, admittedly a bit of a gray area ethically, and one thing had led to another. I now had properties in different locations that were well beyond the reported purchasing power of our person of interest, as well as other evidences of spending that would indicate unreported income at best. Possibly and probably, from my experience, illegal income at that.

Then my reaction to his last bit of information, aside from my feelings of guilt based on my own reticence to share. If someone had pulled the arrow on through Scott's body, and apparently struggled in doing so; who better to show hesitation than a former girlfriend? A girlfriend more interested in an older, more mature professional. Say, a state employed biologist supervising an internship?

In my mind, at least, I was beginning to make a pretty good case for Miss Molly Roberts to be both the fulfiller of a middle-aged pedophile's dreams and the executioner of a high school boy's aspirations and life. Molly Roberts was barely seventeen years of age; a child in spite of her physical presence and emotional worldliness. That made James Middleton a criminal!

Had Scott, the rapidly becoming ex-boyfriend, learned of the affair and threatened Dr. Middleton? Had that got Scott killed? Good thing I had charts and timelines. I was getting away ahead of myself and trying to make facts fit a theory, not the other way around.

Middleton could not have killed Scott. Middleton was murdered first. Back to Miss Molly. By Golly. Had Scott learned of the affair and killed Middleton; Ms. Roberts learned of this crime and in a moment of revenge killed her former boyfriend for his having killed her current one? On the Current?

I needed sleep; was getting punchy. I made out some note cards. Just the facts, Jack. Jack Webb. Web of deceit. I needed sleep now. I would put the cards on the wall tomorrow; decide then where to put them and what if any green string should be strung. String. String 'em up! I drank some warm milk and went to bed.

Chapter Thirty

The reporter had not been happy with the Buddy Stevens interview; neither had the editor of the local paper.

"What's new? What's printable? There's nothing much here to run. I'll look through it later; clean it up. Don't worry; I'll give you the byline." This last said as if seeing his name in print was important. Not for this, the man thought. The military had been so much easier. So many words every week and a few photographs. Not sure if anyone ever read what he'd written. Certainly not the CO that masqueraded as an editor.

The first few months of rehabilitation had been excruciating. Physically and mentally. He had enjoyed the Navy before. The excitement, the out of country experience. Even the limited action he had seen. He loved the adrenaline rush, even in training. Then a visiting Captain, a rushed exercise to impress the Brass and the accident. The corporal that caused his fall was disciplined for his mistake; should have been shot.

The threat of discharge hung over him until his Sergeant, a good guy, noticed a notation in his personnel records about his brief stint on a school newspaper. Bought him enough years for retirement. Now he supplemented a meager pension with his reporting. Just had to keep this editor happy until something better came along. So the interview on a slow news week. Even murders get old when there are no new clues. The fire was new.

Stevens had seemed uptight towards the last of their conversation. His body language was all wrong. Almost more aggressive than annoyed. Had he recognized him from their earlier conversations?

The reporter had worried about this when he first had called to sell the antlers, for he had bought beer and bait at the tackle shop on more than one occasion. It was overhearing some of the conversations during those visits that had put the reporter on the alert for a possible buyer in the first place. But very little about that day had gone well.

To begin with, he had walked far enough from his vehicle that his old injuries were acting up. He had the requisite orange hat and vest over his camouflaged overalls and jacket. Was hoping to fill his unused tag with the large buck that he'd seen in the area during the earlier regular firearms season. This was the Alternative Season. Muzzleloaders. Bows, crossbows, atlatls. And centerfire pistols.

He'd carried his Thompson Contender with the .30-.30 Winchester barrel. With a 1.5-4X Leupold scope and loaded with 150 grain Winchester Power Points he was ready. He was also ready when he saw the huge elk almost stagger into his view. He quickly changed the cartridge in his single-shot bolt action pistol, inserting one of the Remington Accelerators he had kept all these years just for such an occasion. Was somewhat surprised how close he was able to get to the huge animal. With the Accelerator he would have to try for the head.

No longer produced by the North Carolina based corporation, Accelerators had used plastic shims to place much smaller diameter bullets into the brass cartridges for some rifles, including the 30-30 Winchester. The idea was a much lighter, faster projectile. The other result was a bullet with no discernable ballistics, as the plastic shim kept the bullet from physically interacting with the grooves in the barrel of the rifle. Remington had voluntarily ceased their production.

The reporter had bought a hundred rounds while they were still available, anticipating shots like he was about to take. Shots he would not wish traced. The bull had gone down after only staggering another few yards, caught further below the base of the skull than he had intended. The little thrashing was over by the time he'd removed all orange from his body and walked up. The cap and vest he shoved into his daypack while he took out what tools he would soon need.

Here was something he was sure he could sell. The first elk killed in the wilds of Missouri in more than a hundred and fifty years. Just as some rich people horded stolen artwork in basements and private studies just so that they could gloat of their possession; some never even sharing with the closest of confidants, he knew that someone would pay dearly to possess what had not been available for more than a century and a half.

The first hint of trouble was the dart protruding from its rump. Three bright orange fletchings less than a foot forward of its tail. He pulled it out and carefully put it in his pocket. Now what to do with an animal that looked as large as a yearling steer? His legs were hurting, and he was more than a mile from his truck. The Gerber field dressing kit he'd taken from his daypack had a bone-saw. He removed the skullcap and antlers as quickly as possible, knowing there was no way he could carry a caped head that far, let alone hide it if such action became necessary. The antlers could be placed into brush or covered with leaves if he heard someone approaching. With this lighter load he believed he could still make good time.

And he had, worried all the while that there might be some locator device hidden in the dart. He'd put the antlers in the back of his Ford F-150 and covered them with a tarp and driven right down the main highway on the way to his old cabin a couple of miles the other side of town. So far, so good; though he believed the sweat collecting under his clothes was as much from anxiety as from exertion.

He had stored both the dart and the antlers in an old outhouse at an abandoned cabin a half-mile from his own. Left all wrapped in not only the tarp, but covered the packet in leaves and small sticks as if a packrat had built a new home. He had only to make the deal and arrange the transaction. He'd require the money to be dropped off at some remote spot and then a day later he would drop off directions to the rack. The dart he would destroy.

And then that jerk would not buy them. After the initial conversation, would not even return his calls; though to provide the untraceable number he had given him, he had driven more than a hundred miles to buy a burner phone with cash at a crowded truck stop. Subsequent calls within just a few days were blocked.

The reporter wondered what his sarge would do. Though he had at one time a pretty good skill set, and before the accident was in great physical shape; he'd always left strategic thinking to platoon leaders and more experienced non-coms. His last sergeant had been one of the best. The reporter liked taking direction when he knew it was coming from a good man.

He had learned one thing in his military training, by both direct instruction and experienced observation. Sometimes you had to just cut your losses. After all, though he had hoped for and expected a great windfall; what did he have in the packet stored less than a mile away? One afternoon and late evening, some gas and a few bucks for a burner. One expended cartridge. What had even Mr. Buddy Stevens said that one day on the phone? "Somethings just aren't worth the risk." Well, Mr. Stevens, you just might well be right.

Chapter Thirty-One

Bill Haden was worried and did not know what to do. Normally a deliberate man, he was unaccustomed to this feeling. The death, no—the murder, of his nephew had hit him hard. This much time and still no word from the law made him begin to doubt if justice was going to be achieved. For Scott; for him. For the boy's father; his younger brother.

He and his brother had not spoken since the funeral. Not at church, not at either's home. A widower shortly after his marriage, he had no children. His sweet Martha had died in childbirth as had the infant. Scott was as close to a son as he would ever have and it had been a constant source of dissension the lack of time that Robert had spent with the boy. Even Robert's wife had on more than one occasion agreed with Bill, driving the wedge between siblings even deeper.

To pass the time, Bill Haden had turned his attention to the finishing of several chores he had assigned Scott in recent months. The first was repairing some trailers for the upcoming season. Old eight haulers that were still quite serviceable save for bent fenders and broken taillights. Bill had finished these several days ago; not much required as Scott had already re-wired them and replaced the broken lenses. All that was left for him had been the welding of some lost rings where ropes were tied to secure the canoes in transit.

Yesterday Bill had turned his attentions to a paddle shack Scott had begun cleaning a few weeks ago. Broken paddles that needed new blades, cushions and life jackets that required some sewing or being thrown away. The room in the back where wheel bearings and more expensive items were kept. The desk that had been an office during more hectic days and now served to store that which he no longer much thought about.

Among the latter was an old .38 Special Smith & Wesson snub-nosed revolver he would carry when he had to on occasion quiet a rowdy group in his private campground. Over the years more judicious attention to what types of groups he accepted pretty much eliminated that problem, and he had not taken the old gun out for at least ten seasons. He'd oiled it up well after a thorough cleaning and placed it in an oil soaked cloth before putting it back in its original case. Yesterday he had found neither case nor pistol. Looked repeatedly into the same draw in which he knew it had been placed.

No one else had access to that room, as it was kept secured with a padlock. A padlock for which he had given Scott the key scarcely a month ago when the project was first began. His nephew had to have been the one who'd took, no stole, the gun. To sell? To threaten someone? To play that silly tail game, killing and leaving animals to rot in private people's fields? That behavior had been the basis for some harsh words between both his brother and his nephew; his brother believing it was not that serious of a crime.

Should he call Sheriff Barnes? For a moment he even wondered if somehow he himself could get in trouble for not securing it better; then silently chastised himself for such thoughts. Even if he was wrong to have given his nephew access to a weapon, Scott was eighteen and had more than one rifle or shotgun always present in his pickup. Besides, anything that could help find the man that murdered flesh of his flesh had to be done, come hail or hot water!

Chapter Thirty-Two

The call had been short and to the point. The sheriff had first not wished to take it when the desk clerk told him who it was on the phone. He could not imagine the Haden's pain; was well aware that in many ways the older man had been more of a father than the kid's real dad. But he wore a badge and had taken an oath to serve.

"Put him on" he had instructed her.

"Bill, I'm sorry. I don't have anything new. I'm working several angles."

"Joe, I know you are. I've got something for you." The elder Haden proceeded to tell him of the pistol and the old box of ammunition that were both missing. How he had given Scott a key around a month ago; before any of the killings had begun.

"It might not have anything to do with my nephew's death. But maybe, if you can catch somebody for something, maybe things will start to break your way. Good luck and God bless you." With that the man had hung up.

Joe could still hear the grief in the old man's voice, felt he had aged even more rapidly since the boy's murder. If only they could catch someone is right, the tired law officer agreed. He wondered if his own frustration was becoming as palpable as that which he had just listened to on the phone. Wondered if he himself was aging at an accelerated rate. Joe knew someone else that would be interested in this new piece of information. He picked back up the phone and dialed.

Chapter Thirty-Three

Molly put down the phone. Could not believe what she'd just done. The receptionist had been polite and efficient.

"District Office. With whom may I connect you?" The desk clerk was listening to a dial tone as she finished her spiel.

Molly hit the disconnect icon almost immediately after the ringing had stopped and the voice on the other end had begun. What had she been thinking? It had just become so much a habit over the last couple of months. Her internship gave her cover, so she had always felt comfortable calling and asking to speak to James at his office; even in leaving messages when he was in the field. Nothing indiscreet, just "checking on our schedule" or "just wanted to let him know I had finished that assignment."

James would always call her back on her cellphone. Sometimes they talked for hours, especially on weekend evenings when getting up for school or work would not interfere. She believed she could tell him anything. Looked forward to his smiles at work, the touch of his hand when handing out an "atta boy!" The occasional hug.

She fought back the tears as she wrestled with the fact they would never speak again. Her dream, that she would someday be with him always, had ended. Had been shattered by someone she had once thought she could trust. Someone she had made pay.

The call had come late at night. At first she had thought it was James. Then remembered it could not be James; would never again be James. His slurred speech revealed the caller's identity.

"Scott, why are you calling. I've asked you not to. I have a lot on my mind." She had eventually tried to explain that Scott and she might someday again be friends, but that would be all. "I am grieving. Can't you see that?" Molly was not surprised that a kid could not understand the love that she had felt for Dr. Middleton, and basically told him as much.

It was then he had surprised her.

"Do you know what I've done for us? For you? He was an old man, stealing your life. I stopped him" he had almost screamed into the phone before she'd hung up. Had he said "stopped" or "shot" she had then wondered.

Finally, it had come to her. Scott, in some kind of infantile rage, had killed her beloved James. Had torn from her life her hopes and dreams of happiness. Dreams that sustained her, when reality was becoming an ever-darkening set of clouds, invisible to all but her.

Her parent's divorce and her mother's re-marriage had left her home an emotional abyss. It was true that at school she was a popular cheerleader and had several friends male and female alike. But no one she could share with until James had come along. No one that understood that she lived in a world where love and

111

attention was directed between two newlyweds and little spilled over for an adolescent daughter.

Scott had been fun and capable of getting her to laugh; but the joy receded as quickly as the jokes ended. The gifts were nice and for a while she thought filled the void that had become her heart. Then she volunteered and met Dr. Middleton. Became enamored by his competence and attracted to his mature outlook on life. To the good doctor, himself.

Scott had taken this all away. Scott had committed murder and in some fantastical world of self-delusion tried to say it had been for her. Scott was a monster. A real monster. And real monsters had to be stopped.

She'd found the old Bear Whitetail Hunter in the garage. Made sure there were still arrows in the quiver. Her real father had been a hunter. When her mother's infidelity had finally driven him away, he took a rifle and a favored fly rod. Everything else he left behind, save for one suitcase of clothes. His departure had been quick and final. Twelve at the time, she had overheard the secret assignations as well as the heated arguments. Had not been surprised; only heartbroken.

She had shot the bow a time or two over the years; had even gone down to the local range when she turned sixteen and got her driver's license. There they had worked on her form and realigned the sights. Suggested that she get something newer with a more manageable draw.

Molly had overheard Scott and Ronnie that day at school make their plans to meet later that evening, she unobserved behind the door to a friend's locker. Realizing the opportunity, and knowing well Scott's almost compulsive habit of being early, she'd taken the bow and arrows and made her plans.

Scott was already there when she arrived, but did not even bother to turn around. The bow was harder to pull than she remembered; her left arm already shaking before she could make the compound mechanism "break" and reduce the draw strength initially required. Worried that at any moment, her former friend and now hated "victim" could turn around; she released the arrow the moment the top sight pin was between his shoulder blades. Molly was amazed at how much noise came from the shot and started to return to the car. Angst and perhaps a bit of pity made her walk to her dying classmate.

Scott was done jerking by the time she approached the body. On his side, small pink bubbles of froth were escaping his mouth and nostrils. The wheezing she'd first heard was over. His eyes were wide open; the beer still clutched in his now lifeless hand. She remembered that her father had made his own arrows, and often spoke of how easily his friends could identify his shafts when on the range or afield.

She shoved the body against the ground with her left foot, and grasped the protruding arrow in her gloved hands. It came, reluctantly, but came. As she continued to push with her foot, the body rolled from its position on its side to a more flush position with the ground, the new angle causing the arrow to now catch its fletchings and to resist just long enough for Molly's hands to momentarily slip. The blades of the hunting broadhead sliced easily through her right leather glove and into the fleshy parts of her hand and fingers. She got a new grip and finished extracting the murder weapon and hastened to her car.

It was dark enough for any other vehicles to most probably be shining their lights; so, in their absence she believed herself undetected. Still shaking, she started the engine and drove quickly away. Tears clouded her vision as she relived the anger at the murderer of her beloved James, and then continued as she realized she was now herself guilty of that very same crime. Hours would pass before she finally succumbed to sleep.

Chapter Thirty-Four

Buddy was sure he now knew who had killed the elk, and he was pretty sure he knew who had killed Middleton. And he was afraid he knew whom had killed the Hayden kid. He knew Ronnie was wishing to move up in his illegal organization. Had at times expressed his frustrations that it had actually been the pitcher who had brought his fellow ballplayer into "the business."

Scott had been hungrier, willing to take greater risks. Hence Buddy's awarding him with greater opportunities, at least in the "killing field." In the drug business, they were basically equals. Equals who were not expanding their client lists, as both teenage boys generally ran in the same circle of friends and acquaintances.

Buddy had shared some of his concerns about Scott's increased drinking with Ronnie, purposely leaving out his role in the taking of trophy heads. Had also shared earlier his concerns about Middleton with Scott. Had Scott revealed these concerns to Ronnie? Had the more dominant classmate put two and two together? Had Ronnie believed by taking care of the state biologist and his own peer he would be moved up the ladder? And if so, how far could he trust Ronnie? Was there yet another loose end to be closed? And, if so, how?

What Buddy did not know was Middleton had in fact come to his demise by the hands of one of his protégés; it just was not

Ronnie. Scott had been present the day of the Corp biologist's visit; had remembered where Buddy had stuck the card under the corner of his cash register.

Scott had called the home number penciled on the back late at night, using a coat sleeve to muffle and disguise his voice. Had promised the older man information about the elk killing, insisting he meet him at an old river crossing still attainable by four-wheel drive and to do so alone at midnight. The anonymous call seemed to have included enough detail to be legit. Middleton had arrived at Beal Landing moments before the day was to officially come to an end. More than a half-hour earlier, Scott had already parked at Log Yard and walked down.

Dr. James Middleton heard the cocking of the revolver and had just started to turn when the .38 caliber bullet entered his left side. Already a soft-nose meant to expand, Scott had further assured its degradation by his own knife cuts made to the quite malleable lead. Middleton was still breathing when Scott drug him into the edge of the stream. The gigging party would find him the following evening on an exposed gravel bar less than a mile above Paint Rock Bluff. Crows had already found him shortly after daylight.

Buddy knew only of the finding; could only speculate the how and why. Like so many who had chosen such similar pathways, he attributed the cause to material greed as that was the only motive he himself understood. He knew nothing of the passions of love nor even jealousy; envy was as close as he could come.

He did, again like many walking those darker paths of life, understand fear. Fear and self-preservation. Any drugs he'd had on hand were long disbursed along that network of dealers and users. The trophy heads had been burned. He was still unsure to what degree of threat the remaining high schooler was; Ronnie's motives and actions somewhat predictable and therefore still susceptible to manipulation. Execution was still an option.

The one surety was the danger posed by the want-to-be antler salesman. The man interested in Buddy's "other sidelines." The reporter. He had to go. When Buddy had recognized the voice, the phrasing; he feared he had given something away in his reaction. Perhaps not, but there was no sense taking a chance. It would not be the first time he'd taken life to secure his own future, Buddy thought as he began making plans.

Chapter Thirty-Five

Only a few miles from all that is left of the Bait & Tackle shop, mainly the one building; another person of similar ilk was making his own plans. He hadn't the years of living outside the law that Mr. Buddy Stevens possessed, but had his own particular set of skills and experiences. Some of the more recent experiences he himself had been trying to forget.

He, too, had a strong belief in self-preservation. A belief more recently accompanied by a willingness to walk outside even the vaguest of laws and now totally with absolutely no element of guidance from a superior of any kind. Unlike the smirk so often worn by Mr. Stevens, his countenance was almost devoid of expression. His eyes, similarly devoid of life.

Chapter Thirty-Six

Ronnie was nervous as he exited his car and walked into the local coffee shop. At Molly's urging, he'd agreed to meet with this lawyer who was asking so many questions about the rash of crime that had invaded the serenity of their hometown in recent weeks. His high school friend, the government biologist and of course the elk mutilations that had started it all. The crime spree was now being referred to as "the elk killings."

He agreed to the meeting in part because he feared in the not too distant future he would possibly be needing the services of a good attorney, and thought he should at least know one. He also thought, that if he let her do most of the talking, he might find out more of where the investigation stood and was heading than could be gleaned from any of the media sources. She was already seated in a booth when he entered.

"How are you doing?" she'd begun, going on to explain her concern about the loss of his friend. That was the last question to which he'd elaborated. He had shared some of his sense of loss; did his best to mask his feelings of guilt. They'd talked some of his ball playing; the lawyer seeming to be genuinely concerned with his pain.

Then the interrogation began; at least that's how he would later describe it to Buddy. "Did he know about poaching?" "Were he and Scott involved in this 'tail' game?" "Did he know anyone that had a grudge against Scott? Dr. Middleton?" "What did he know about drugs in the local communities?"

Ronnie had merely shaken his head "No!" for many of the responses. At times, he would verbalize his reply, but in monosyllabic words and abbreviated sentences. He felt on trial, but recognized this was largely due to his feelings of guilt along with his growing fears of prosecution.

Molly was outside waiting when it was over. A cold wind blew through the January sky and she invited him to her car to escape from the cold. He declined; feigning anger at her for suggesting what had just taken place. All too aware that such anger was actually directed at himself and at his own complicity in all that had happened.

He'd retreated to the warmth of his own pickup truck and headed out to Buddy's place. They had not spoken for some time, and again he felt awkward entering a business. Buddy greeted him with a cold beer and a slap on the back.

"Been too long!" Buddy offered cordially. "We've got plenty of work to do; money to make. Let me know when you're ready!" Ronnie stayed for an hour; sharing more silence than conversation. What talking was done had focused on the cold front that had moved into the southern part of the state and what seasons

were still in. After a bit, Ronnie left; promising to be in touch soon.
Both knew it to be a lie.

As Ronnie drove away, himself trying to decide on a course
of action; Buddy was doing the same. Realizing his relationship
with this young man could never go back to what it had been,
because of guilt, perhaps, and the kid's need to find someone beside
himself to blame; Buddy continued perfecting plans of his own.
Permanent plans, he smiled to himself. Once more the smirk.
Terminal plans, he decided. He almost laughed.

Chapter Thirty-Seven

I found myself already immersed in tax problems; those of clients and not my own. It had been nearly a month and no arrests had been made. I welcomed the call from my newfound friend, Ranger Mark Williams. This time he'd offered to provide the refreshments, but still wished to come to my abode—mainly, he insisted, because of the "wall."

Not that my notes were limited to only one side of that spare-bedroom, but the interior one with the most room had the green twine and the supposed connections. We'd even began posting pictures of suspects. I hoped that tonight would be the night we closed at least part of this case. Hoped, also, that I would enjoy whatever varmint Ranger Williams had brought to be reheated in my humble kitchen.

I was pleasantly surprised; it was venison stew, with lots of vegetables. "Something to stick to our ribs" as we were thinking, Mark explained. Between our hunger and our anxiousness to get to the case, the meal was short. The night was long.

By midnight, we'd gone over pictures of the crime scenes he'd been copied from all other agencies involved. We read reports from State Police as well as witness statements from them and the Corps Game Wardens. Some of what I was seeing was most likely not intended for a civilian's eyes; officer of the court or not. I had just stood up, ready to call it a night, when something in the corner of a black and white shot of a gravel bar caught my eye.

Mark was staring at part of an autopsy report on a windowed wall as I began to speak. "I've got it!" I announced, only it was his voice saying the exact same words that I'd just heard. He was beaming. "I've got it!" he repeated, as I tried to do the same. Now he had heard me.

"Go ahead" he encouraged, though he seemed to be about to burst with his own deduction, having just realized another possibility for the facts before him.

"No. Please, you first" I came back.

"No, really. Go ahead. Your house; your wall."

I was kind of glad he had not resorted to that "ladies go first" thing, for reasons of which I am unsure. "My house" I could handle.

"Molly killed Scott. Look at this corner of the photo. That's a decorative strap off the boots she was wearing when we spoke. I recognized that part of her one boot looked torn; I believe the left one. She was there; I'm sure of it." I was almost giddy, afraid before now to condemn a young girl because of rumors, speculation and coincidence.

"You're right" Mark agreed. "The hesitation on retrieving the arrow. At first I thought Ronnie, because of the friendship. But it was more physical than mental. When the arrow was pulled

123

loose, the angle of the body shifted. The arrow would have had a fair amount of weight pressing it against the rib cage it had just nicked. It was a failure of strength, not of spirit."

We agreed that the cuts on Molly's hands could be matched to the murder weapon if and when it was ever located. Even the remnants of fletching found inside the corpse might very well have some of Molly's DNA still adhered to them. We had finally solved the mystery murder. We had figured it out.

Except for the "Why" and then of course, there was still the "Who" killed Dr. Middleton. That all came later.

Chapter Thirty-Eight

Sheriff Barnes met the two would-be sleuths for breakfast. Ranger Williams and Rachel Hunt assured him they had cracked the case. They shared the Molly Roberts' theory, as well as the rest of their conclusions. For they had more. After all, success breeds success.

There had been an inappropriate relationship between the young girl and her mentor. Obviously, it had gone south and Molly had found herself rejected. She took the gun from Scott's uncle's place, presumably during one of her and Scott's assignations, and dispatched the pedophile who had so wrongly used her. Luring him to a remote spot for a final degradation was probably easy.

Somehow, Scott had figured it out and confronted his classmate and former girlfriend. Cowardly, but effectively, she had dispatched him with a bow. Likely the one her long gone father had taught her to shoot as a child. More than likely from a hidden ambush, almost out of range. Hence the arrow not clearing the body. It was in trying to retrieve the arrow that somehow she had lost the decorative strap from her leather boot.

Joe Barnes sat there taking a few notes, mostly just listening.

"Plenty for a warrant. Good work." The accolade was more than they'd expected; the warrant the hoped-for prize. Both

125

Williams and Hunt agreed to accompany the Sherriff to his office to assist in filling in any gaps for the arrest warrant. Each taking their own separate vehicles, the procession soon arrived at the Courthouse. Ranger Williams had been on the radio, briefing his fellow officers on the direction of the investigation, when the Sherriff broke in on the Park's frequency.

"Mark, I'm sending one of my uniforms to the river to try and find that strap. You come on to the office. We have another body."

"What about Ms. Hunt?" the Park Ranger asked. "Want her to come on as well or head home for now?"

"Load her up and bring her along. We're headed to the mouth of Carr Creek. We might need those attentive eyes again." The Sherriff was already back in his Tahoe and headed out as Mark explained the situation to Rachel.

"Why me?" Rachel asked, though as she was finishing her inquiry she was already buckling up.

"I guess Joe figures we make a good team. Anyway, here we go. This might not be pretty."

Ranger Williams knew there was a big difference between crime scene photos, no matter how gruesome, and an actual crime scene. He said a silent prayer as he headed back towards Current River. For the loss of life, for those who would be mourning, and asked again for the strength to "do the green and gray" proud.

The ranger considered wearing the uniform of any law enforcement agency an honor, and sought always to express such belief through his actions. He also asked that, "if it be His will"; the scene Rachel was about to witness would not be too horrific.

Though his mind was racing over "who's" and "why's" once again, he remained quiet throughout the drive. In his career, he'd pulled too many bodies from this body of water; generally due to drowning. Still, murder was different. And murder, it again was; for he'd heard Joe refer to "another victim" when assigning deputies to the crime scene.

Chapter Thirty-Nine

Buddy was annoyed with the feeling he just wasn't getting something; much like when that last mosquito of the season continues to buzz around your back porch. You can't see it; don't always hear it. But you know it's there. Such was his feeling about the recent rash of crime. He knew a fair amount, but there was too much he did not know.

He knew of his own complicity, of course. He was fairly sure of who had killed young Scott. He now even had an idea of who had taken care of the biologist. These had been inconveniences to his business, true; but the real blow had been the killing of the elk. That had cost him big money; had left him to renege on a promised delivery. That was the criminal he wished to catch, and that was the identity that eluded him.

That is until this interview. Buddy now remembered where and when he had heard similar phrasing. That reporter.

"What other sidelines are you in?" That had been the phrase. The anonymous antler peddler and the reporter had both used "sidelines" in their inquiries. Buddy now knew who had "muddied his water." All that was left now was to decide what to do and then do it.

A phone call later, the meeting was set. A price had been agreed upon; a place chosen for the exchange. He laughed about his choice of meeting places----Polecat Hollow! Somehow Buddy believed this all so appropriate. He considered the man that had butchered what should have been a trophy animal, even more importantly had destroyed an ongoing live source of revenue; well, the reporter was a "polecat." An animal that stunk up his surroundings. And Buddy knew quite well the deserved fate of any nuisance polecat.

Chapter Forty

The crime scene was actually upstream from the mouth of Carr Creek, off a gravel road through private property to the mouth of Spring Hollow. Once a community store, the old concrete block building had been remodeled into a private residence used seasonably by the owners. The victim was about a quarter mile up a trail into what was known as Polecat Hollow. Or, to be precise; the head of the victim.

Computer monitored video surveillance of the residence had noted suspicious movement; hence the call to the Sherriff's Department, hence the find. Already on the scene was one of the family and a County Deputy who had been closer to the somewhat remote area. And the reporter. Again, he'd picked up the transmission on his own monitor and was already taking notes. His camera remained in his vehicle per law enforcement request.

Set atop an outcropping of rock was the head of what had up until late last night been Mr. Buddy Stevens. Not just his head, but what would be determined later to be the attached skin from his upper torso. He had been caped, much as a trophy animal. Blood splatter and bits of gore supported the fact that this was indeed the murder scene; though the body would be found scattered throughout the side hollows of Cardareva Mountain over the next several weeks. A few parts were never recovered.

Rachel and Mark joined the sheriff in surveying the scene, taking care not to interfere with the work of the forensic team that had been called in from the capitol and would arrive shortly. They were allowed to take pictures; at least Mark was and he took direction and advice from Rachel as he did so. Both took notes.

Once the state lab boys were on the scene, Joe indicated to Mark he was headed back to the County Courthouse to procure the arrest warrant they had originally sought. Mark explained to Rachel what was happening as he held the door for her. Once on the road, they sat in silence for only a brief few moments; then returned to their list of suspects. Anxious to hear what the Roberts girl would have to say, neither believed her capable of this most recent and by far most gruesome crime.

Mark again became silent, this time as he went once more to his Lord in prayer. Nothing had prepared him for what he had just seen, and he was beginning to believe Satan himself was walking these hills he'd called home since first being assigned here what now felt like a century ago.

Rachel was lost for the moment in her own contemplations. Kipling and Morrow had only hinted at such savagery. Only Tolstoy had ever put such carnage into words. She felt once more physically ill, and hoped that she would not have to ask Mark to pull over for her to be sick.

Joe Barnes was mad, and as usual in such mood, had to watch himself to keep from speeding. It had long been one of his pet peeves that so many officers of the law routinely abused both speed limits and fellow officers' forbearance. He purposely slowed back to the posted limit, knowing that the warrant would be waiting as would young Miss Molly.

The sheriff wanted desperately to solve this case; to stop these atrocities. Still cognizant of the election later that coming fall, this had gone far beyond politics. He'd been paid to protect the people of this county. He was well aware of his failures, and had begun taking steps with neighboring rescue units to see they did not occur again. The deaths of the two hikers in particular haunted him.

But now he had a monster loose in their midst, and could only wonder if his lack of enforcement of some of what he considered the "lesser laws" had not led to this. This is what happened in Third World Countries. Maybe Detroit or Chicago. Los Angeles. Not the Ozarks. This was what he was thinking as he parked his vehicle and entered his office.

Chapter Forty-One

The Roberts' arrest warrant was assigned to a deputy and a female clerk; both instructed to simply and politely as possible bring the girl in for questioning. The deputy assigned had earlier found the remnant of leather noticed by Ms. Hunt in the photograph, and had tagged and bagged it as evidence. The warrant he was carrying was accompanied by another to search the young lady's residence for the leather boots Ms. Hunt recalled the teenage girl wearing in their meeting what seemed so long ago.

Sheriff Barnes and his "sidekicks" (for that is how he was beginning to consider the tall park ranger and diminutive lawyer) were executing another warrant to search the premises of the recently deceased Mr. Stevens; this based on an anonymous call suggesting they do so. What they found was interesting. Hate mail from more than one disgruntled buyer, along with records of transactions of several illegal mounts. Oddly, these were all typewritten, possibly from the same computer. Certainly, they were all the same font.

The proverbial "smoking gun" was the antlers. Fourteen magnificent points and part of the skullcap. One of the letters had referred to their non-delivery. The situation looked obvious. Some very sick buyer had had all of Buddy's obfuscation he could handle and snapped; killing the illegal trafficker and treating him as one of his wild prey. Barnes hoped that whoever did this was from out of state and was now done with his county. He hoped forensics could possibly pick something up from the letters that would allow some other police force to apprehend the fiend and bring him to justice.

Now, he and the rest of his trio were once more headed to his office where Joe looked forward to finally confronting at least one of the killers. The "duo's" theory had made sense and with the evidence they were amassing, he hoped for a confession.

Chapter Forty-Two

I had just got out of a hot shower and was drinking a cup of tea. Maybe tax bills and spreadsheets would look good when I went to the office in the morning. The late morning. In the past few days I had seen more gore than I could have previously imagined. I had to admit I got caught up in the adrenalin rush of chasing "bad guys." Had enjoyed spending time with Mark and hearing his stories of when the Park Service manned a blacksmith shop and had made sorghum molasses for tourists to enjoy. Was inspired by his tales of the guided fishing trips of the previous century.

But I was worn out physically as well as mentally. The final straw had not been the head and skin cape greeting us on that ledge, as heinous as that had been. It was how terribly wrong we were about the murders. I had viewed Molly as a victim, of both mental anguish and most probably statutory rape. Hers had not been the actions of someone trying to regain some sense of control in her life.

She admitted to the murder of Scott Haden, her fellow classmate and former boyfriend. She had not killed him to cover up her murder of Dr. Middleton for using her. Scott had killed the good doctor to free Molly from his influence. She had killed Scott simply as revenge. When confronted with the evidence of the leather strap and its match to the boots found in her closet, she admitted all.

Molly directed the sheriff's people to where she had hidden the bow and the arrows, including the one that had cut her hand as she pulled it from the teenager's chest. She was very much in love with the late biologist; assured us all that she was sure that he had loved her in return.

No, they had never physically consummated the relationship. In fact, they had never even kissed. Still, she was sure of his love. I was still in shock as to how wrong Mark and I had been. Not all was in waste, though. Scott's killer was in custody because of our work, and I guess, my observation. And the mystery of Dr. Middleton's death was solved, and his killer now beyond prosecution; certainly, no longer a threat to society.

And the elk mutilation was at last solved, with only Buddy Stevens' killer left at large; and the sheriff was fairly sure that person was no longer a danger to any locals. As I sipped my tea, I began reading the article that summarized for the public much of what I had been privy to hours before.

The reporter had finally sold a front page, above the fold news story. It included the crime scenes, the carnage. The anonymous tip that led the sheriff and his men to that almost forgotten hollow. Even listed the hate letters that could be found. Though run with no gory pictures; it did describe the murder scene and the crime in detail. Down to the fact that a human had been beheaded and caped, the spine severed with the same type of bone saw that had been used to remove the antlers from the imperial elk just shy of a month before. The article was succinct and authoritative.

Molly's confession was included, leaked before legal counsel reminded her to be quiet. Somehow, she believed it's telling might win some sympathy with potential jurors. She was pleading diminished capacity because of unrequited love. A love that she was sure would have blossomed into marriage to the bachelor biologist, if only they'd been given more time.

I put the paper down and scratched the noble head resting lovingly on my thigh. Rex had been so patient and supportive during this, for lack of a better term, adventure. I promised to take him for a good long walk in the morning before heading off to the office.

Heading off. Off with their heads. Off with Buddy's head. I was punchy and needing sleep. Then it hit me. I didn't even bother to look at the clock when I called Mark.

Chapter Forty-Three

Sheriff Barnes and Ranger Mark Williams served the warrants at approximately 3:00 a.m. the following morning. They were accompanied by four deputies, three other Park Rangers and a SWAT team provided by the state police. Flash bangs and tear gas were launched into the somewhat isolated cabin; none of the distant neighbors were awakened by the noise. There was no firefight; the suspect was dead on the scene, victim of a self-inflicted gunshot to the head.

The printer matched the letters found at the Stevens residence. The bone saw had been washed and was back in the black case with Gerber imprinted on it in silver. DNA residue from both the elk's skullcap and Stevens' spine were still present.

I was at the courthouse when I got the call. Was glad no officers had been put in danger. Was glad that now it was all over. The clue had been the reference to the saw. I, as well as the police, had always referred to the antlers as being removed by a chainsaw. Only the real elk murderer would have known the truth.

I had been reading a document that was to be copied to Miss Molly Roberts. It was a final Will and Testament and she was listed as a beneficiary. The part pertinent to her read as follows:

"and to my assistant and co-worker from these past several months, I leave a trust fund of $60,000 to be used for college tuition, dorm room and board when and if she continues to pursue a career in Environmental Biology. Miss Molly Roberts has been like the daughter I never had and I hope this persuades her to fulfill this dream she so often shared in our talks. I will miss such moments so."

Seems the good doctor had been diagnosed with aggressive Stage Five cancer that was untreatable. He'd told no one, but had only months ago changed his will to provide this enticement to a young person he'd enjoyed mentoring. A young lady he thought of as a daughter. I could think of no greater compliment; no greater love. I feared Miss Roberts would take the news differently.

Postscript

This book goes to press almost a full year after the real-life incident that inspired it. A trophy bull elk was killed and mutilated near the Current River the night of December 28, 2015. To date there have been no productive leads. MDC officials may still be reached at Operation Game Thief Hotline 1-800-392-1111.

Brandon Butler, Executive Director of the Conservation Federation of Missouri made an important point with his following analogy: "You've likely read a headline that stated 'Hunter Shoots Deer in Park.' Well, no; a poacher shot a deer in the park. Think of it like this; if you walk into a bank and withdraw money you are a customer. If you walk into a bank with a gun and demand money, you are a robber. There is a big difference between taking legally and taking illegally. Hunters take legally. Poachers take illegally."

It is my fervent hope that this book inspires more of us to step up and be the moral examples to our youth in all aspects of our lives, certainly including our behaviors afield.

I also hope that it initiates further conversation about our game laws and penalties for poaching, along with the "farming" of wild animals. Such game ranches have at times actually saved endangered species and can provide real hunting opportunities; however careful monitoring is a must.

I hope that you enjoyed this little mystery, and you look for the upcoming volume, *The Cave Springs Conspiracy,* where you can rejoin Ms. Rachel Hunt and Ranger Mark Williams as together they once again work to solve another mystery in the Ozarks.

About the Author

Rick Mansfield is an avid outdoorsmen, where he gets much of the inspiration for his stories. Along with a weekly syndicated column, *Reflections from the Road,* Rick does storytelling in historical costume as well as hosts numerous river clean-ups and gives presentations about Christian stewardship.

Rick resides on a small farm outside Ellington, MO with his wife Judy and two dogs—Big D and Dharma. Rick's activities may be followed on Facebook page –**Rick Mansfield** as well as Facebook page—**Stewards of the Ozarks**.

Rick is a retired educator and volunteer preacher and welcomes any and all opportunities to address the public-especially our youth. Rick may be reached at <u>emansfield2004@yahoo.com</u> or 573-663-2269 or

Rick Mansfield, 701 CR 602, Ellington, MO 63638

Other books by Rick Mansfield:

D'Ya Want A Possum? And Other Ozark Salutations

Kids, Crafts, & Christ: A Collection of Games and Things

A Riverman's Legacy And Other Ozark Tales

Ozark Sayings, Doings, And Just Plain Ol' Ponderings

Coming soon:

Huck Don't Care! A Dog's Path to a Better Life

The Commentary Boat

Still Waters and Forgotten Hollows

Christmas in Coon Hollow

The Two Deaths of Black Tom Moss

I Believe in You

The Commentary Boat

The Cave Springs Conspiracy (another Rachel Hunt mystery)

Sales of Rick's books go to support the Ozark Heritage Project and the Stewards of the Ozarks. OHP is a non-profit 501 c3 (EIN 46-1849-249) so any and all contributions are tax deductible. In 2016, OHP hosted three river clean-ups on the Current River, Jacks Fork and their tributaries and collected more than four tons of trash from these beautiful waters. OHP co-hosted a two-day event with the National Park Service/Ozark National Scenic Riverways that cleaned more than 125 miles of streams within their borders. OHP provided food, entertainment and support service for the event.

OHP is currently also working on the preservation of two historic structures and is always in need of both volunteers and monetary support. Again, we thank you for the purchase of this book and the support that will provide OHP in the future. Have a blessed day!

Rick Mansfield— Historic Storyteller

To the left dressed as "C.W." Nichols, a river guide with decades of experience speaking from 1967, shown with vintage Current River guide boat. The display includes a boat, guide chair, cook box and old metallined wooden cooler complete with bottle opener.

C.W. can speak of the history of guiding on Ozark streams as well as the displacement of property and culture caused by the creation of the Ozark National Scenic Riverways, along with other important events of that era—nationally as well as locally.

Below is Nick Walker, a reporter from the late 19th or early 20th century. He can talk knowledgeably about the history of newspapers during that time, as well as any historic events they covered. To aid his recollection, it is asked that preferred topics be given him in advance. Building of our roads and infrastructure are popular topics, as well as finances and postal service.

Last is "Runt" Johnson. A teamster or bullwalker from the 1890's to the early 20th century. His favorite topics include the settling of the Midwest, the wagon trains that went on westward, and the beginning of our railroads as well as bus system.

All of these can teach a myriad of subjects within these themes—math, environmental science, language arts and of course history. The great advantage of these presentations is that they are being told first person as they were happening. This greatly allows for increased audience participation and listener interest. Specific course objectives will be addressed if given beforehand.

Dr. Eric "Rick" Mansfield is a seasoned educator and utilizes his training and experience in tailoring his presentation to the audience. Business audiences can be addressed as well.

Fees are negotiable and inexpensive, especially when Rick may also sell his books. Rick's organization —

Ozark Heritage Project—is a tax deductible non-profit so assistance from local businesses is often easily attained.

Dr. Mansfield may also instruct in his own identity, hosting river and field clean-ups and other environmentally and socially positive activities to help with our young generation. Applicable lessons of stewardship and social responsibility are offered in an interesting and uplifting manner. Go to Rick Mansfield's Facebook page to follow many of his organization's activities.

Rick may be reached at (573) 663-2269, emansfield2004@yahoo.com or

Rick Mansfield, Ozark Heritage Project
701 CR 602
Ellington, MO 63638

A great use of Rick's time is to book him for the whole school day and use him in multiple classrooms. If interested, he can then also present to parent groups that evening. Rick is currently already booking for 2017. Please schedule early and send requested objectives or requirements. Thanks!

Made in the USA
Middletown, DE
15 May 2017